The Forester Fortune

by

Harry Calvert

The Seider Press, La Groudiere

The right of Harry Calvert to be identified as the author of **The Forester Fortune** has been asserted by him under Copyright Amendment (Moral Rights) Act 2000.

All rights reserved.

Copyright © Harry Calvert 2018.

ISBN: 978-0-244-96719-2

This book is a work of fiction. Names, characters, businesses, organisations, places, events and incidents are either the product of the author's imagination or used fictitiously. Any resemblance to actual persons living or dead, events or places is entirely coincidental.

No part of this publication may be reproduced, stored in or introduced into a retrieval system or transmitted by any other form or by any means without the prior written consent of the author. Also, this book may not be hired out whether for a fee or otherwise in any cover other than supplied by the author.

To Heather, for very good reasons.

CHAPTER ONE

No-one seems to know exactly when Foresters' started brewing. It must have been in the second half of the nineteenth century; there are no records before that. Initially, the brewing was for personal consumption only. There were hundreds in Burton who did this; something magic, apparently, about the waters of the River Trent unlikely though this may seem.

It was Elsie Forester who concocted the first brew, in the back kitchen of their terrace house just off the Stone Road. It was initially just a small beer – low alcohol and safer to drink than the local water. But it soon acquired a charm of its own and the family drank it not so much for protection as for pleasure.

Foresters' ale must have had an edge on some of the others because, first the neighbours, then others farther afield started to buy it from the Foresters. When pubs round about found their customers asking for "Forester's" instead of the pub's own brew, they too found themselves reluctantly obliged to stock it or lose the trade.

As further orders from local pubs came in it soon became obvious that premises more suitable than the back kitchen of a terrace house were desirable so, using the increasing profits from what had not started out as a business, the Foresters first bought larger premises then slowly equipped them bit by bit and the first Forester's Brewery came into being headed by Thomas Forester. Once the brewing had became a profitable proposition, the men had taken over from Elsie and "Foresters" became "Forest Ale" with wholly unwarranted overtones of sylvan calm.

When John Forester, Thomas's grandson, conceived his formula for "Forest Fine" he hoped it would be a modest success. The Forester brewery, one of many similar breweries in the town, paid its way with its main brew, Forest Ale, now found in a couple of dozen pubs in and around the local area. But John wanted something better – a prestige ale. This was not only a matter of brewery pride; he calculated, rightly in the event, that his customers would be willing to pay a penny more for a pint that was that bit better. And enough of his customers were.

Unfortunately, so was John himself. Aged only fifty-eight, ironically he fell victim to cirrhosis of the liver and the business passed to his son, Peter, then aged thirty-four. Forest Fine continued to thrive and expansion of the brewery became necessary. Peter managed to acquire at a knock-down price the premises of another nearby brewery undergoing hard times and the new premises became devoted entirely to the production of Forest Fine.

There was always, of course, the risk that none

of this would last and Peter wisely decided that limiting liability was a good idea. He incorporated the business all the shares but one remaining with him. The brewery's solicitor acted as company secretary and held one share.

Far from declining, sales of Forest Fine continued to surge and within three years it had become a nationwide brand. Yet greater capacity was necessary and Peter managed once more to acquire a more or less defunct nearby brewery at a give-away price. Two years thereafter he decided it was time for the company to go public. The issue was oversubscribed and Peter walked away with a generous contract to continue as Chief Executive Officer of the company for a further two years and twenty-four million pounds. Almost a million pounds of this was immediately spent on building a large country house near the golf course.

Although at that time no such tree was to be seen, poplars were duly planted to line the driveway. The house became "The Poplars" and remains in the family at the present day. A further ninety thousand pounds was lavished on a small old *manoir* in need of some care and attention in the Vire Valley in northern France.

"The Poplars" was an appropriately grand house with Palladian overtones. It contained four large reception rooms, one furnished as a study although there had been little evidence so far of any such activity in the Forester family. The first floor offered four large double bedrooms and two bathrooms – the day of the ensuite was yet to become commonplace. Attic space provided accommodation for servants with access via a separate staircase leading from the kitchen area. Outside, a stable block was built with a groom's loft, which, in the event, was never used for that purpose. The same fate attended the construction of a garage block for three cars. The garages were rarely used for their intended purpose and became storehouses of one sort or another, the family's cars usually being parked in the large courtyard at the side of the house.

Improving the *manoir* was left to local, French, workers. It turned out to be a more expensive undertaking than had been anticipated, partly because there was more to do than had been foreseen, partly because the cost of doing it was inflated by the greed almost approaching dishonesty of the local craftsmen employed for the purpose – an absentee owner was easy pickings. But money really didn't matter all that much to the Foresters.

When he was only twenty-two, Peter had met Rosalie who ran a gift shop in the town. Until then, his flirtations had been casual and short-lived. He had gone into Rosalie's shop to buy a present for his mother's birthday. Rosalie knew him by sight in the same way that she knew almost everyone in town by sight but had never met him. She was impressed by him. The small talk and smiles they exchanged were slightly more personal than those normally accompanying a commercial transaction and Peter spent more than enough on his mother's present in order to make an impression on Rosalie.

Rosalie was ten years Peter's senior. She had enjoyed many relationships but nothing had come of any of them. She had not wanted it to. She had a good life – loved her horses - and was far from desperate to get married but time was moving on and she was aware of nearing the shelf. Peter was a handsome young man and they exchanged pleasantries. He was clearly intelligent and well-to-do and his smile accompanied an obvious sense of humour. She took to him immediately.

His knowledge of her was less even than hers of him. He knew she ran the shop but that was all. He now became really aware of her for the first time. She was mature but she was still beautiful and he became interested in her as more than a shop owner almost straight away on that first meeting. He invited her out to dinner; she accepted and things developed from there. It was a love match.

There was no surprise in his proposal of marriage to her or in her acceptance of it. When he announced the news to his parents their reservations were obvious. He was very young, too young, they thought, to be taking such a step. And she was ten years older than he but he was clearly serious about the matter. They invited Rosalie to dinner and their reservations soon dissolved. So all was set.

There was no reason for delay. They were married just twelve weeks later in the local parish church. In the course of the twelve weeks, Peter exchanged contracts for the sale of a large, detached mock-Tudor house on a sizable plot in the suburbs which was to become their home for nearly eleven years. The house was his parents' wedding gift.

They had been married less than a year when their first child, Alexandra, arrived. A mere thirteen months after that, a second daughter, Katherine, was born. The arrival of Alex posed a problem for Rosalie's business; obviously, she could no longer run it full-time but she did not wish to give it up. It was a hobby as well as a business and gave her a measure of independence, which she was reluctant to surrender.

It was not a serious problem. She had a part-time assistant whose youngest child had just entered the sixth form and she was more than happy to work full-time. In effect, she and Rosalie exchanged roles. This obviously reduced the profits of the business but this did not matter. Rosalie was no longer dependant on it. This arrangement became even more necessary two years after Kate was born when George arrived. His being the result of a miscalculation did nothing to abate the demands made on Rosalie's time though Peter, of course, being a busy man, was much less affected by the birth.

When they were old enough, first Alex and then Kate were enrolled in the local independent preparatory school for girls where it soon became obvious that they were highly promising pupils. From here, they proceeded, one after the other, to Jevington, an independent girls school some fifty miles south of the town. It was sufficiently accessible for them to return home not only for vacations but also at whatever weekends and for whatever special occasions they chose. As the years wore on and school friendships and activities developed, these returns home became less and less frequent and eventually were restricted to some special occasions and vacations only.

George's education proved more problematic. He too, in his turn, was enrolled in a local independent preparatory school, then in The Birches, a second-rate public school not far from Jevington. He proved to be unnecessarily ignorant, "unnecessarily" because the chief cause was idleness, not stupidity although he was clearly less bright than both girls.

The girls were only ten and eleven and George only eight when their grandfather died. The mock-Tudor residence was sold and the family moved into The Poplars. A mere seven years later, they lost their father in a road accident. Since the sale of the business and the end of his two-year contract as CEO,

Peter had used his newfound leisure to fit in a round of golf almost every day but he spent possibly too much time at the nineteenth hole. He had headed off back down the lane in his Mercedes coupe, taken a bend too fast and reacted too slowly to avoid both an oncoming car and a very large and solid oak tree. He avoided the oncoming car but not the oak. He had not bothered to fix his seatbelt – it was less than a mile back to The Poplars. He went through the windscreen and hit the tree headfirst.

He died instantly.

Under his will Rosalie received ten million pounds absolutely. Alex, Kate and George each received a million pounds in trust, such of the income as the trustees allowed being theirs until attaining the age of twenty-one when, unless the trustees objected for good reason, the principal sum became theirs absolutely. The trustees treated the three children equally and generously. At age sixteen, each received £25,000 per annum until attaining majority. Rosalie, having received an inheritance which more than met her needs (and, indeed, desires), and anxious to ensure that the children were properly set up, arranged for a second million pounds out of her inheritance to be put in trust for each of the children on the same terms as the legacies.

The rest of the estate, some fifteen million pounds, was placed in a trust for Rosalie to enjoy the income for life and then, on her death, for Alex, Kate and George equally to become theirs absolutely on attaining the age of twenty-one again provided the trustees did not reasonably object.

Although Rosalie, intent on ensuring that they appreciated the facts of financial life, insisted that they contribute to household expenses, what remained of their incomes was quite enough to disabuse all three children of the notion that there would come a point where earning a living was a necessary activity.

As expected, Alex and Kate did well at school each excelling in A-level results in successive years. Alex went to Cambridge to read medicine. Kate joined the rare band of people who turn down a place at Oxford and went to Imperial College where she read engineering and then architecture. Upon qualifying, Alex worked in a London hospital for four years then emigrated to British Columbia where she eventually secured a permanent place in a hospital in Vancouver as an orthopaedic surgeon. Alex had, throughout their joint lives, always occupied a large space in Kate's awareness. It was not much of an exaggeration, looked at from Kate's point of view, to think of them as a single entity. After this break between Alex and Kate, things would never quite be the same again. For Kate, in particular, it left a void in her life which was never adequately filled.

Upon qualifying, Kate joined a firm of architects in Birmingham. She found herself employed, as the newest person in the business, on various undemanding tasks such as designing extensions to suburban semi-detached houses. She was bored to tears. This was not what she had had in mind. She was, furthermore, less than contented with her treatment by some of the more senior members of the firm. She was even, on one occasion, asked to make coffee by the son of one of the founding partners of the firm. Her "make it yourself. What do you think I am? I'm not your skivvy" did not go down well. The prospect of an eventual partnership became more distant.

Had she needed the money, she would have had to stick it out. She did not, and after two years resigned to start her own firm from scratch. She was asked to enter into a restrictive covenant preventing her from poaching the firm's clients but she refused. They should have thought of it sooner. Had she needed the money, she might have been tempted by the offer of six months' severance pay but she did not.

She found premises just outside the centre on her own side of the city. They offered a ground floor, which gave the newly established firm a visible presence on the high street and two further floors. One constituted additional work space; the other was a penthouse flat into which she moved, quitting "The Poplars" for good and relieving her of a cumbersome and time-consuming commute from there.

Circumstances would later dictate another move to a detached Edwardian house overlooking the park.

She managed to poach from her ex-employers only two clients for whom she had worked and the benefits of that soon faded. One was a one-off project for the design of a conversion of a large house into flats and once the job was done, that was it. The second contract was prematurely terminated almost immediately. The clients' cash-flow problems ensured that they were put into liquidation by the Revenue and that put an end to that contract as well. No further immediate benefit accrued from her previous employment. It was now entirely up to her although she was, of course, unlikely to starve.

Kate initially worked completely on her own, even attending to her own clerical and secretarial needs. Word spreading among family and friends, however, gradually brought in enough work for her to cover costs even though more staff were employed. Within three years, it had become a sound business and she employed her first professional assistant, James Connelly, just graduated from Leeds. He was able and pleasant and became as much a friend as an employee. There was never any inkling of a romantic connection. Connelly and his girlfriend, who moved with him to Birmingham, had been together since their second year and were destined shortly to marry and start a family.

Without Connelly's help, the firm might not

have made the great leap forward. It was he who spotted the competition for the design of a new hotel complex to be developed and run by a large building firm, Blake Construction, in Dubai and his help in preparing their submission was substantial. When, after a wait of several months, the news broke that they had won, he became Kate's business partner.

The Dubai hotel complex was a highly ambitious project. It constituted the development of a site just a few miles up the coast from the centre of the city. It was to consist of thirty super-luxurious suites, including two "Royal suites" each suite served by its own butler and the Royal suites by a maid as well. A free chauffeur service at the disposal of guests would take them to any chosen destination on demand. A restaurant targeted at three Michelin stars would provide the "hautest" of cuisines. That part of the site unoccupied by buildings was to consist of water and foliage, each suite having its own swimming pool and garden.

A part of the extensive site, to be screened off by palm trees, would contain a pumping station, a desalination plant, stores, garaging for the vehicles and accommodation for one hundred and twenty staff, largely in small single rooms. It was going to cost a lot of money. Andrew Blake, head of Blake Construction and seeking to diversify, considered they could afford it but it was a risky venture.

Winning this contract established Kate's firm's

reputation and led to a positive flood of other contracts, one of them also in the Gulf. It had set her on the road not only to professional success but also to greater wealth than she already possessed.

Success in the competition followed by the rapid intake of business led to the situation where, suddenly, everyone wanted to employ Forester & Connelly. As a consequence, the firm expanded rapidly. It was Forester's Brewery all over again. A division of labour was established. Kate decided to concentrate on the Dubai contracts whilst James, assisted by two new recently-graduated assistants, took charge of the rest.

CHAPTER TWO

The Dubai contract initially necessitated frequent trips sometimes involving lengthy stays in that city. On the first of these trips she met Andrew Blake whose projected new hotel complex had been the subject of the competition. He was a striking-looking man and, due to meticulous, almost vain, grooming looked much younger than his actual forty-six years in appearance.

Blake Construction had been established by his father as a small-time building firm but it was Andrew who had been the driving force behind its expansion. He had early on spotted opportunities stemming from the use of oil money to promote massive growth in the Gulf and, after winning Blake's first contract there and coming to appreciate the possibilities more fully, he had established a new branch of the firm there. It eventually became the major branch of the business and Blake moved out to Dubai and set up home there. His wife refused to accompany him and kept on their house in Kent with the predictable event that their marriage suffered.

Kate was unattached. She had never married. She had had the customary rash of affairs at university but had since been too preoccupied in her work to bother much with men. Blake's first marriage, when he was thirty-four years old, had not survived his move to Dubai and he had been divorced after only three years. There were no children, the main reason being that Blake detested them.

On Kate's first visit to Dubai after securing the contract, her Emirates flight arrived at 7:30 p.m. on the Monday evening. She arrived at the airport, negotiated the border, collected her bag and headed for the exit. There she was, as she had been told to expect to be, greeted by one Dr. Sally Begum. Who this person was Kate did not know. She appeared to be Indian, or Pakistani; something sub-continental. Having registered the colour of her skin Kate awaited further explanation.

In a chauffeur-driven company Range Rover on the way to a very good hotel where she was to be accommodated during her stay, Dr. Begum introduced herself as Director of Materials and Logistics of Blake Construction. Kate wondered what her background was. She seemed urbane; her English accent betrayed no foreign influence. She seemed about the same age as Kate (Dr. Begum was, in fact, five years older but wearing better) and it struck Kate, as somewhat surprising that "one of them" should hold what was apparently a very responsible position at such an early age. There had been a few of "them" at Jevington — daughters, probably of Pakistani traders who had made a lot of money selling shoddy clothing in markets such as that in Burton. They always kept themselves to themselves, didn't mix. It never occurred to Kate that her set didn't mix either.

The Range Rover duly delivered them to the hotel. Dr. Begum did not hang about. She confirmed the arrangements for the next day – a meeting with Andrew Blake at 7:00 a.m.; the chauffeur-driven Range Rover would collect her - and left.

7:00 a.m.! Kate was not aware that such an hour existed.

She had a poor night's sleep. Midnight in Dubai was, after all, only tea-time according to her internal clock. When she arose at 6:00 a.m., the same clock was registering bed-time. She showered and dressed – although she would have to cope with desert heat, she nevertheless opted for a dark grey skirt and jacket, white blouse, heels and some discreet but nevertheless obviously expensive jewellery. First impressions mattered.

She had a light breakfast. The same chauffeur awaited her with the same Range Rover at the main entrance to the hotel. He must work a long day, she thought. They headed off to Blake Construction – its modest premises, shortly to be expanded according to plans by Forester and Connelly, were in fact just around the corner.

Entering, Kate was escorted to the first floor and ushered into Andrew Blake's outer office. His secretary informed him of her arrival and showed her immediately into his private suite. He had come around his desk and met her at the door. A warm handshake lasted perhaps a little longer than necessary. The smiles exchanged were possibly a little warmer than required. It may have been far from love at first sight, but it was something out of the same box. It was certainly the case that at that moment the day's business was not uppermost in their mind of either of them.

They had dinner together that evening. Her hotel had a very good restaurant. By the end of the meal, the cause of their business had been little advanced but they had learned a great deal about each other's lives – marital history, career history, interests etc. At the end of the meal neither wished to break up the pleasant occasion. Kate contemplated inviting him up to her room. She was surprised to admit to herself that she would have liked that, but thought it much too premature and presumptuous. When the conversation turned to his Dubai home, however, she ventured:

"It sounds absolutely lovely. I'd love to see it sometime."

This elicited the entirely unsurprising response "I'd love to show it to you," and, after the shortest of pauses "Why not now? Unless you're too tired, that is. I suppose you are – long flight, busy day…"

He gave her abundant excuses to decline without offending but she did not take the opportunity and he did take the implication.

"No, I feel fine." She replied. "I suppose it will

all catch up with me later but I'm OK at the moment."

"Great; let's go then. I might even manage to rustle up a bottle of legally dubious fizz."

The Range Rover (still the same chauffeur – did he sleep in the car?) was waiting. They drove a few miles to the coast until the car turned off the road and up a short drive to a large, adobe-type house, which fronted on the beach.

They entered. The lights were already on and they were greeted by some sort of servant who produced on demand a bottle of cooled champagne on the terrace overlooking the sea. After one glass, and without pouring a second, Andrew said:

"Come on. I'll show you the rest of the house," picking up the bottle and continuing, pointedly, "bring your glass."

They got as far as the bedroom, immediately embraced and kissed one another passionately. She had not had sex for a long-time and had never engaged in it on a first date, but she now wanted it almost desperately, as if to make up for lost time. It was only much later that she learned that he had not suffered the same deprivation.

They set about undressing one another and were soon on the bed naked. He was a good lover and at the same time as being excitedly aroused by his attention she found herself regretting her abstinence. It was the best sex she had ever had.

The unplanned nature of the encounter and a

failure of communication meant that they took no precautions. He assumed she was on the pill; she assumed he would wear a condom. Neither assumption was warranted.

The business side of the relationship occupied them for the whole of the next day, although Kate found it more difficult than usual to concentrate on the matter in hand. It took a continuing conscious effort to hide the fact that they were now connected by more than business. Such an effort could not be wholly successful. The chauffeur, who actually had slept in the Range Rover all night, could hardly be unaware and it was not at all certain that the Director of Materials and Logistics had no inkling of what had taken place.

As soon as could be, on her return to Birmingham, Kate discovered that she was pregnant. She had mixed feelings. She had always like the idea of having a daughter (she was sure it would be a daughter; she did not want a son) at some unspecified time in the future. She had never reconciled herself to Alex's departure. Time was moving on and perhaps that future had now arrived. What Andrew's reaction to the news would be she could not imagine, nor did she much care.

She found out on her next visit to the Gulf, which, in the event, was scheduled to take place only six days after she became sure of her condition. Her news occasioned him no joy. He did not want, had never wanted, children but the inevitable confronted him when she insisted adamantly that an abortion was out of the question. He had no choice but to accept the fact. Kate succeeded in overcoming his reluctance to embrace the consequences. Yes, he finally accepted, they would have to get married – give the child a father. The idea was not without its merits. He imagined eventually handing over the business to a son and there would be considerable commercial benefits in the merger of Blake Construction and Forester & Connelly.

One person, whilst appreciating the merits of a business merger, disliked intensely the prospect of the personal one – Dr. Sally Begum or, as Kate was to come to refer to her later, once fully-informed of the situation, "that Paki bitch".

It was not a particularly apt designation. Dr. Begum was a third generation immigrant from India into the United Kingdom. Her grandfather had served in the British army in the Second World War, attaining the rank of captain and he and his wife, in part because of as yet ill-formed fears about the prospects for Muslims in an independent India, had decided to stay in the United Kingdom. There were no immigration difficulties in those days. Their son had become a doctor and his daughter; Sally (the name itself a clear indication of the measure of integration) had so far enjoyed a highly successful career. An M.Sc. in Oxford had been followed by a

20

D.Phil. in Construction Engineering in a prestigious American University. She had not anticipated living in Dubai but when the opportunity had come along to join Blake Construction there it had been too good to miss. Andrew Blake had soon recognised her qualities and she had risen (some said reclined) rapidly to her present position in the firm.

Dr. Begum's professional qualities were not the only ones recognised by Andrew Blake. He was not a celibate and, shortly after divorce from his first wife, established a liaison with Dr. Begum. She had not been reluctant to add the status of mistress to her other roles. She had no expectation but she did have hope that this status might eventually mature into marriage but it was never mentioned between them. She thought it was probably the case that his experience of that institution thus far had left him bruised and disinclined to entertain a repetition; she hoped that time might heal the wounds. The wounds had apparently healed more quickly than she had anticipated and the announcement of Kate and Andrew's wedding had been a shock. It also provoked a hostility towards Kate, which would not easily, indeed never, be abated.

Dr. Begum attended their wedding and made all the appropriate noises. She did, however, speculate that the formation of this new partnership by Andrew might not necessarily involve the breaking up of the existing one with her and in this she proved correct.

Andrew was more or less permanently resident in Dubai. Kate's business kept her in the United Kingdom. As a consequence they saw little of each other, a price worth paying, they had decided, in order eventually to finance an early retirement and a very comfortable life together back in Europe. As the contract in Dubai progressed, her professional visits became less frequent. His to the United Kingdom were rare. Once she gave birth, her visits ceased entirely except for one visit, which provoked divorce and another, seminal, last visit, by which time their marriage had been dissolved.

The marriage, such as it was, worked for a time. It was almost as soon as legitimately could be that she gave birth to their son, Tom, but he was far from being exclusively a source of joy to her. On the contrary, caring for him posed an additional strain on an already over-busy life. She was bitterly disappointed that the child was a boy and to this was now added the inevitable breakdown of her marriage.

Absence had not made the heart grow fonder and on her penultimate visit, shortly after Tom was born, presence made it grow markedly less so.

It was primarily a business visit and the business involved Dr. Begum's department. She joined them for lunch at the hotel. Although, ostensibly, only business was on the agenda, it was inevitable, given the triangle present, that other items should surface.

Nothing was overt but, intentionally or not, Dr. Begum's attitude towards Andrew – the momentary smiles directed only at him; one or two anecdotes which referred to experiences which only Andrew and Dr. Begum had shared – suddenly prompted Kate to wonder if their relationship was confined to business. Surely that was unlikely - Dr. Begum was, after all, of a different race.

Once the business was done, Dr. Begum had no pretext to hang about and left the husband and wife at the table together. It was not long before Kate ventured:

"Sally seemed very friendly."

"Yes, of course. I consider her a friend; we've been working here together for over two years. What's your point?"

Never one to beat about the bush, Kate leapt straight in:

"Are you having an affair with her?"

"Christ almighty! What sort of a question is that?"

"I notice you're not denying it."

"Of course I deny it. I'm married to you now…"

"'Now'. That's interesting. And before we were married…?"

"What's that got to do with anything? I'm married to you. That's that."

"Is it? You seem to be implying that before I came along you were having an affair with her."

"So what if I was. Have you never had an affair... before we were married?"

"So you were having an affair with her."

"YES. Now can we talk about something else?"

"What about now. When I'm away, I mean. Now that we are married; do you ever see her, the Paki bitch?

"Cut that out. Her name's Sally."

"Sally bitch, then, do you ever go out; have dinner; when I'm not here?"

"What's wrong with that?"

"Nothing if that's all there is to it... But it isn't is it?"

Andrew foolishly lost his temper. "For fuck's sake, you're away for months at a time. You expect me to live like a monk – celibate?"

"Yes, actually, I do," said Kate and got up and left the table. "I'll be staying here tonight. I would appreciate it if we could tie up the loose business ends first thing tomorrow. I want to get back as soon as possible. I shall be instituting divorce proceedings."

The tying up of the loose ends unfortunately involved the three of them, in Andrew's office suite. Kate was there early. Sally walked in with a cheery "Good morning." Kate ignored this and launched straight in:

"I gather you've been shagging my husband."

Andrew tried, ineffectually, to intervene. Sally spoke over him:

"Yes," she said, "long before you appeared on the scene and probably after you're long gone, since you ask."

Kate stood to leave. "James will be over to finish the business. I hope profoundly never to see Dubai, or either of you two, again."

It was a dramatic exit, perhaps spoiled by her having to wait for a flight for five hours at the airport. The chauffeur seemed to know what was going on and bid her a fond and final farewell. Kate retained at least one friend in Dubai. But she left behind her a deadly enemy.

Kate always flew business class. On this last occasion, she had found herself seated next to an advocate from Edinburgh who had been in Dubai negotiating the terms of a multi-million pound contract. She had been in a foul mood, angry and offended, and had responded very curtly to his initial approach. He introduced himself.

"Hello, I'm Alexander… Alex," and held out a hand. She was compelled to take it:

"Hello, I'm Kate," she muttered reluctantly, adding, neutrally, "you have the same name as my sister" and turned to the magazine proffered by the flight attendant. Alex, however, was thick-skinned or determined or both for he ignored this and sought to continue the conversation:

"You don't find many girls called Alexander," he said and, when this provoked the most minimal of smiles, continued. He was on his way back to Edinburgh, etc., where was she going? What had she been doing in Dubai...? And she had been compelled to take notice of him. He must have been about her age and was rather good-looking with an engaging smile. Eventually, he had suggested a bottle of champagne. At that point she had the choice of declining or accepting. The events of the two days in Dubai flashed across her mind. She chose to accept.

As the champagne disappeared, so more personal facts emerged. Both were married, with one child. Alex sympathised when she told him that her marriage had just ended. They shared a bottle of Menetou Salon blanc with dinner – it was an eight-hour flight and they would not be landing until late evening. He was staying overnight at a Heathrow hotel, catching a flight to Edinburgh early the following morning. She told him that she intended to catch a late train to Birmingham.

"What time do you expect to arrive home?" he asked.

"Oh, I don't know... early hours, I suppose."

"You should stay overnight and head back first thing tomorrow."

She understood perfectly. She decided to stay overnight.

"What hotel are you in?" she asked.

"I have a suite at the Hilton," he informed her, adding, as she had expected, now even hoped, "You can share it, if you like."

She looked at him quizzically but did not hesitate for long. "That's very kind of you. I will, if I may."

She would have found it very hard to describe her motivations. Primarily, he was a very attractive man and it was a fair time since she had confronted the prospect of a fuck with such enthusiasm. But it would also, she conceived, put one over on the "Paki bitch" and, just possibly, if she handled it right, give her the daughter she craved. She did not much care who the father was.

They collected their bags and took a taxi for the short drive to the hotel. Once in the suite, they said little. Both undressed and took showers one after the other. She climbed into bed naked and he soon joined her in the same state. There was little conversation.

"Are you protected?" he asked.

"Yes," she lied. It made no difference. In the event, no pregnancy resulted.

When she awoke the following morning, he was gone. He left no message. It dawned on her that she only knew his first name and had no idea how to contact him, but that did not matter. She had no intention of doing so. She packed her things, made sure he had paid the bill, left the hotel, took a taxi to the station and arrived in Birmingham in time to pay a quick visit to the office, then have lunch with James before returning home.

There, awful news awaited her. Her mother informed her that Alex, her sister in British Columbia, had breast cancer. The news had arrived while Kate had been in the air and attempts to contact her had failed. The prognosis was unclear. The cancer was not of the worst possible kind but neither was it of the sort which inspires confidence in a cure. Alex was planning to come over to visit family and friends as soon as an interval in her treatment allowed, probably in several months time. It might or might not be for the last time. At the end of her visit, Rosalie would return with Alex to British Columbia and remain there for however long it took for Alex to recover – or worse. In the event, Rosalie remained in Vancouver for much longer than had been expected before the disease eventually triumphed by which time, Kate's "daughter" was well settled in her new home.

CHAPTER THREE

Only one child died as a result of the outbreak of meningitis at Parkhead Primary School. That was Mollie Ferguson. Most parents affected were frightened for a time, then relieved, then forgot all about it. For Mollie's parents, Karen and Sean, particularly Karen, it seemed that life would never be the same again.

This view was, of course, correct. Life never would be the same again, especially for Karen. It would consist of enduring unprecedented pain into which would be filtered, bit-by-bit, a new reality. In Karen's case, the pain was heightened; it had taken years for her to conceive the daughter she craved only to have her brutally wrenched away. Apart from anything else it was strikingly unjust. There were four hundred children in the school and only one had died. Why did it have to be hers?

There is, they say, something unique in every person who ever walked the earth. Perhaps – but it would be hard to find in the cases of Karen and Sean Ferguson. They both came from and continued to belong to that mass of humanity, which we call the working class, as though it were an odd sort of substance filling space on the surface of the earth. They had attended the same comprehensive school at Barford. There, they were aware of each other but there was no sort of attachment during their school days.

Karen was an almost anonymous pupil. She did the minimum of work, not an iota more or less, and made no demands. Had she worked just a bit harder the C/Ds which she obtained in her GCSEs might have been B/Cs and her life might have taken a totally different path but school work was not encouraged at home. Her parents regarded education as a troublesome imposition forced upon them by the state – the very opposite of the view embraced by their own parents, that school offered a great boon – an opportunity for children to escape the life that enslaved their forebears.

It never entered Karen's, or anyone else's reckoning, that she might move into the sixth form with a view to progressing to some form of higher education. Her family needed the money and she left school as soon as she could and found a job straight away stacking shelves on the lowest wage in a brand-new supermarket just opened on the outskirts of the town. She had made a success of it and by the time Mollie had come along she had been promoted to supervisor earning a commensurately increased salary.

Sean had trodden a remarkably similar path. His led initially to working as a fitter in a local firm of tyre and exhaust suppliers. He, too, had been promoted – to foreman, again with a hike in his wages.

Although they knew one another at school, it was only after both had left that they became more familiar. This was the result of frequenting "The Panther's Lair" in the town on Saturday nights. It seemed like an odd name until you discovered that its owner/operator was a modest entrepreneur of West Indian origin named Marcus Lucius Panther.

The Panther's Lair was the destination of choice of the vast majority of the gilded youth of Barford. It led to a sexual encounter of some sort (almost always short of actually fucking) for Karen most Saturday nights, not always in the most sophisticated of circumstances (usually as one of a number of couples about their business at the back of the premises.) Sean inhabited the same environment.

You would not describe Karen as beautiful but she was pretty enough and took care of herself up to a point. Unfortunately, beyond that point lay a diet of largely fatty food. The default evening meal was from the local fish and chip shop where, usually, a deep-fried sausage or burger accompanied a mountain of chips. This produced its inevitable effect and Karen, whilst not exactly obese, was perhaps a stone heavier than she should have been. It did not deter Sean.

Sean's parents, Roman Catholics, had moved from Northern Ireland before Sean was born, looking for work. He was the eldest of five children and although he made good progress it was considered highly desirable that he too leave school and contribute to the family's finances as soon as possible, hence his career. Both in school and once he left, Sean's main interest in life was sex (which occupied most of his Confessions), followed by soccer, expressed first in playing for the school, then in support for Birmingham City. To these interests, once out of school, he added beer and cigarettes.

He was not as dull as this range of interests suggests. He was not stupid. He had a great sense of humour and his erstwhile prowess at soccer made him an eligible catch. It was several years after both had left school that he and Karen noticed one another again at the Panther's Lair. They spent an increasing amount of time together, both on the dance-floor and at the back. It was no surprise that they started "going together" eventually getting engaged. Karen was not a Roman Catholic but was quite willing to do whatever was necessary to meet the requirements of Sean's family and duly did so, so that was no problem.

They were married as soon as could be arranged after the preliminaries were gone through. They were only twenty years old, but there seemed to be no point in just hanging around to reach a more appropriate age. And, more specifically, Karen wanted to get on with the business of having a family, apparently the chief ambition of most of her mates at school.

In this respect, they had mixed success. The

first conception resulted in a miscarriage, but the second yielded a daughter, Mollie. All attempts to add to Mollie failed and she was still their only child when she fell victim to the meningitis at six years old.

Even before Mollie's death Karen and Sean had begun to wonder if further children were to be denied them. After her death, they found themselves wondering if they were destined to be childless. It was almost surreal (although the Ferguson parents were in no doubt that Divine intervention was at work) that Karen became pregnant as a result of their first sexual encounter after Mollie's funeral. This pregnancy yielded a son, Seamus, doubly precious and extremely cherished. Almost three years later, a daughter, Sonya, was added to the family.

By this time, both parents had earned their promotions and, after some ups and downs, things were looking good. Sean went to the pub a couple of nights a week and had also developed a passion for Sudoku which occupied any time not pre-empted by sport on television on his evenings at home. Karen met with friends for morning coffee during her maternity leaves and for a drink, Bingo or both one night a week. In their first four years together, and with some help from parents, they managed to save the 5% deposit, which in those days sufficed, enabling them to purchase a modest terrace house in the inner suburbs.

It had been a very hard week at the office for Katherine Forester (she had cast off "Blake" with its owner) and that was on top of all the other stresses she was currently enduring. She did not have a cold and a headache for no reason. Her marriage, now dissolved, had yielded little more than a son she did not particularly want. That made unwelcome demands on her time, though such demands could be partially met by throwing money at them in the form of a full-time carer.

That was not all. Although the firm was thriving, there was a problem with one particular, large, contract. They were complaining about poor planning of the plumbing installations and insisted that they had specified larger windows overlooking a terrace, so they said, in spite of all evidence to the contrary. The truth of it was that there was nothing to any of these complaints. They had cash-flow problems and were frantically trying to delay staged payments in order to avoid going into liquidation. But none of this eased the burden imposed on Kate in dealing with their complaints and trying to assist in their survival, none of which should have been her problem.

And even all this was as nothing when it came to Alex, her sister. Some two months previously, Rosalie, their mother, had informed her that Alex's condition had worsened. It was now less clear that she would recover. Alex and her mother had decided to return "home" for a few weeks in order for Alex to meet up with old friends, particularly Kate, possibly for the last time. In the event, it did, indeed, prove to be the last time.

Alex died not long after returning to Vancouver. Kate had flown out for the funeral and accompanied her mother on the journey back but the rite of burial had not discharged its intended function and Kate was quite unable to put Alex's death behind her. She found it hard to take work seriously. Fortunately James was willing and able to pick up burdens, which should have been hers. She found Tom even more irritating and was even considering employing a live-in nanny so as to relieve herself of the already reduced onus of bringing up her unwanted son.

Alex's death utterly devastated Kate. Alex had been more than a sister; she had been her other half although this was not a sentiment which was reciprocated. It had been harsh enough when Alex had moved to British Columbia but at least they were able to keep in touch by letter and phone and visit one another occasionally. Now all that was gone and Kate felt strangely isolated and alone.

And brother George had been the very opposite of compensation for the loss of a female soul mate.

He was, of course, a man – that was one thing. But he had turned out to be a singularly unattractive man. He had made nothing of his school career and, once he had reached the minimum school leaving age, had no interest in pursuing education further. Despite his mother's entreaties, he quit school. Whilst their legacies had been the making of Alex and Kate his had had the opposite effect. Although family history initially earned him a job at Forester's that soon fell prey to lateness and absenteeism.

Thereafter, he made no attempt to find work. He did not need to earn. He lived for next to nothing at The Poplars and even before attaining his majority; the income on his legacy enabled him to afford the life-style he chose. It was a life-style involving sex, drink, drugs and company that persuaded the trustees to withhold the transfer of the capital of his legacy for two years but, after two years they relented and, from an already low base, George's career had plummeted even further. From using drugs, he progressed to dealing in them and, after a second conviction, had ended up serving a short term in a young offenders' institution which occupied the site of an old Borstal not too far from The Poplars. It did not seem likely that he would turn his life around. On the contrary, in spite of all his mother's efforts, he had again been arrested, tried, convicted and sentenced to a longer spell at Her Majesty's Pleasure.

He was due to be released from this latest

spell of imprisonment that very day and that added to Kate's acute discomfort. She had no idea what he was going to do on his release. She knew that their mother, Rosalie, had washed her hands of George as, indeed, had she. But bad pennies do turn up and pose problems. She feared that his release might turn out to be problematic for her and she was unsettled as to what her reaction might and should be, if their paths were now to cross again. She needed the weekend to get her breath back.

All this was weighing on Kate's mind as she stuffed a couple of files in her brief-case, pulled on her camel coat and headed off down to the basement garage. She got into the driving seat of the silver Audi A7 and headed off to pick up Tom from the carer. There, she fixed him in his car seat and set off for home. Driving down Powell Street, she noticed the pharmacy on the left, next to the corner shop, rounded the corner and parked immediately on the left. Leaving Tom in his car-seat she strode back to the pharmacy, entered, and bought a variety of medicines and placebos which she considered her condition to warrant – a mixture ostensibly for coughs and colds, some ibuprofen, a bottle of something calculated to cure her cold as she slept (which, even if it did nothing else, would at least knock her out for the night). She paid in cash.

Karen had finished her shift late at the supermarket. It meant a welcome bit of overtime but it also meant she would be late collecting Seamus and Sonya from her mother's and that meant a row. She pulled on her coat and almost sprinted for the bus.

As expected, her mother was in a foul mood by reason of her daughter's lateness. She did not get paid for overtime; indeed, she did not get paid at all.

As soon as she reasonably could, Karen put Sonya in the pram, took Seamus by the hand and set off to walk home, three blocks away. Making her way down Powell Street, the corner shop reminded her that in her rush to pick up the children she had forgotten to pick up milk (irritatingly at a discounted price!) at the supermarket. She parked the pram outside the shop, and, placing Seamus's hand firmly on the handle, ordered him "Now you stay there; keep hold of the pram. Don't move; don't let go. I'll only be a minute."

She entered the shop. There were few customers. She went to the cool cupboard and quickly selected a two-litre bottle of blue-top. The she remembered that she also needed bread and went to the back of the shop to find a loaf of wholemeal. She had to search for it; irritatingly, it never seemed to be in the same place. Eventually, she found it and headed to the checkout where she found herself behind one of the few customers in the place, apparently doing the entire weeks' shopping.

38

She tapped her feet impatiently and sought to glance out of the front window but, as always, it was covered in advertisements.

Kate emerged from the pharmacy and immediately noticed the pram outside the corner-shop. She looked in, smiling at the baby.

"What's the baby's name?" she asked the small boy holding on to the handle of the pram. Seamus replied, returning her smile:

"Sonya," he told the nice lady.

"Hello, Sonya," she said, still smiling, as she picked up the baby and walked off, rounding the corner and, placing it in the footwell of the passenger seat of the A7, drove off.

Karen finally reached the till, paid her bill and exited the shop. She froze. There was Seamus, still gripping the handle of an empty pram. She pulled the blankets back, hoping the baby had somehow slipped down under the coverings. It took her some moments to grasp the situation.

"Where's Sonya? Where's the baby?" she almost screamed at Seamus.

"A nice lady took her. She took her round the

corner," he innocently replied.

"What do you mean 'a nice lady took her'? Why didn't you stop her?"

Poor Seamus could not have done anything right. "You told me to hold on to the pram. I did. I called you but you didn't come."

Panic set in. Karen screamed. "Somebody's stolen my baby." She ran round the corner but by this time the Audi A7 was two miles down the road. She ran back. The shopkeeper was outside; a passer-by had stopped. Somebody rang 999. A passing woman, grasping the situation, sought to console Karen, inevitably to no effect. The police arrived within minutes. Hardly anybody, other than Seamus, had seen anything, and Seamus's report did not help much. A pedestrian on the main street had seen a woman driving off in a "flashy car".

"What kind of car was it?" a police constable asked.

"I don't know. But it was a light colour, grey or white, I think."

"You didn't get the registration number?"

"No, I didn't think."

"Any of it. Can you remember any of it?"

"Sorry, no."

"What about the woman. What was she like?"

"She was just a woman. Middle-aged, I think. A light-brown coat."

"That's all you can remember?"

"Sorry, yes. I didn't realise there was anything wrong."

It did not help much to put out a call for a "flashy car" heading south along Whitchurch road driven by a woman especially since Kate had already reached the motorway and was on her way around Birmingham heading for the north of the city. Although when it eventually made the news it made headlines that took some little time. Long before that, the crime had become effectively insoluble, at least for the time being.

Kate had astonished and frightened herself. On an impulse that lasted no more than two seconds, she had found and abducted her "daughter". She was immediately aware of what she had done and coolly realised that she could not undo it. Even if she turned round immediately and headed back to Powell Street she would still end up being prosecuted for abduction and even if her recantation mitigated her sentence, and she could not be sure of that, she would still end up convicted of a serious and notorious crime and her reputation – and probably her business – would be ruined.

And above all, she had a daughter – the daughter she craved.

She coolly calculated what needed to be done. Creating a new reality in her head, she drove into a large retail park to the north the city. There, although she already had a large amount of cash in her purse, she first visited the ATM and took out the maximum amount. She then went into a vast department store and bought a pram, which became a carrycot, which could be used as a car seat. Although she already had a stock of Tom's baby clothes she bought new things for the new baby, napkins and, with striking foresight, the cheapest bassinet available. It was to be used for only three nights then stored in the garage for a more than a decade and a half.

In the supermarket next door, she bought a range of baby-foods and bottles – she was not sure how old the baby was nor what its diet currently consisted of. She would have to guess but formula ought to be ok. For all these items, she paid cash. Then, after checking on Tom and her new daughter, both of whom were asleep in the car, went into a furniture shop and bought a single bed and mattress, a wardrobe and a chest of drawers cash payable on delivery the following day. Tom would have his own, new, room. The as-yet-unnamed daughter would take over the nursery.

Heading back to the car with her new purchases in the pram topped by the bassinet, she piled everything into the boot and set off for home where she arrived fifteen minutes later. She took no notice of the Mercedes parked just up the road. Why would she? She unloaded the Audi, taking the bassinet into the house. It, ironically named "Tether's

42

End" by a previous owner, was a large, detached Edwardian house with a long drive and large garden, which she had purchased shortly after Tom's birth. The bassinet would be used only until Tom's new room was furnished. After that, it was stored in the garage where it remained for all those years until it was again needed. She took the rest of the things into the house, then fetched Tom and the baby.

Kate normally planned things carefully. Now her unaccustomed impetuosity had left her with a host of problems, which she had, by reason of her lack of foresight, not anticipated but which nevertheless had to be dealt with. She would have to be able to offer explanations to a variety of people for the sudden addition of a new member of the family or take steps to ensure that no explanation was necessary.

In the house, the first thing she did was to phone her carer saying no more than that an unanticipated change of circumstances meant that her services would no longer be required. She undertook to pay for three months care in compensation – a ridiculously generous offer, but she could afford it. She then tried to ring a nanny-agency but got no reply. She had to wait until the Monday to contact them but was then able to secure the employment of a live-in nanny to start forthwith. She was hired simply on the basis of the agency's recommendation. If unsatisfactory, she could be immediately replaced.

In the event, the nanny, a twenty-two year old Portuguese girl named Vittoria who had been in the country two years and whose English was perfectly adequate for the purpose turned out to be more than merely satisfactory. She in turn was more than content with the attic rooms and a bathroom, reached by a separate staircase from the kitchen, which were to become her home for many years. Kate required only that she be reasonably quiet and discreet. Subject to this, she could do as she pleased with her own suite of rooms which Kate was willing, up to a point, to furnish to Vittoria's tastes.

Neither of them anticipated that it would be an arrangement, which would last nearly two decades.

Kate phoned James on the Sunday and informed him that she would be unable to get to work for a few days. She did not explain why. He asked after her health and was reassured. He did not enquire further. Her absence would pose no insoluble problems. She then drove to Burton to see her mother at "The Poplars".

Dealing with her mother was altogether more problematic. She started out by claiming that the baby was actually hers, conceived and born whilst her mother was in British Columbia with Alex. She had kept it from her mother because she thought she had enough on her plate but Rosalie could not credit that.

Kate would, would she not, have certainly let her know that she was pregnant, especially as the birth drew near. There was a long silence, then Rosalie said, "It's the abducted baby, isn't it? The baby in Powell Street in Birmingham. It was you, wasn't it?"

It was almost a relief to Kate to admit it. She had almost lost control of the complex agglomeration of lies she had been obliged to tell.

"What on earth did you think you were doing?" her mother asked, continuing, "You'll go to prison, you know; it's a very serious matter. The best thing you can do now is to put things right straightaway. Phone the police now and get it over with. That's your best chance of minimising the damage."

"There's no 'minimising the damage'. I'm in deep shit whether I return it or not. Even if I were to return it, the only question would be how long I would get. I'd be ruined whatever. I'm not giving the child back."

"What?"

"You heard. I'm going to keep the baby. No-one knows it's me… except, now, you. Are you going to phone the police? Hand me in…!"

Rosalie hesitated. Then "what about those poor parents? How could you do that to them?"

"I didn't think about it. I didn't plan it, you know; it was just some stupid impulse. But they're probably just working class layabouts. Probably have ten children; won't miss the odd one! I didn't mean them any harm, but once you've done it, that's it; there's no going back."

"There is, isn't there. You should pick up that phone now..."

"I've told you, I'm going to keep the baby. It's all arranged. You phone the police if you want to, but you know what it will mean. A long spell in prison for me. I'd have to give up the business." Then, in a vicious moment "How will your coffee mornings go, do you think – three children, one dead, two criminals?"

There was a long pause, then Rosalie said, "You're a heartless bitch, aren't you? I hate it, saying that of my own daughter, but it's true, isn't it? It will come out, eventually, you know that."

"No, I don't. It's all wrapped up very nicely. She's Alex's baby and I have taken her on now the Alex is dead. You brought her back from Canada. That's the story so far as friends and colleagues are concerned."

"It would be easy to blow a hole in that one if anyone ever cottoned on, wouldn't it?"

"Why would anyone 'cotton on'? My sister, unmarried, dies, leaves a baby and I, her sister, take it on. What could be more normal?"

There was a silence. Then her mother heaved a sigh. "Do what you want, but don't expect any help from me. If ever anyone comes asking, I shall tell them what I know; then you really will be in deep shit. And while we're about it, you may have gained your daughter, but I have not gained a granddaughter. It's your problem; I want nothing to do with it."

Kate experienced an inward sigh of relief. "You're not going to report it, then?"

An intake of breath followed a longish silence, then Rosalie capitulated. "No, you know I'm not. How could I send my own daughter to prison?"

So if anyone asked, it was Alex's baby and Kate and Rosalie were bringing it up now that Alex was dead. That was the story Kate would tell James. It was the story they told George next time they saw him some months later though he seemed strangely sceptical about it. It was a story, which could easily be blown out of the water if the crunch came. Alex had not been married, not been pregnant. There was no record of her having given birth or of a baby taking a transatlantic flight.

It was a story, which would also inconsistent with the birth certificate, which Kate hoped, would be obtained albeit in a dubious manner. But, if all else failed, that was the story they would have to stand by. Kate had at first thought that she had organised everything extremely efficiently. Now she was far from sure and although, as time went on, she gradually acquired a greater reassurance, she was never wholly comfortable with her mendacious new status.

But she had got what she wanted.

It had not been a pleasant exchange. Kate's relationship with her mother was irreparably damaged. Visits to "The Poplars" became rare and were only allowed if Kate went on her own or with Tom. Rosalie persisted in this for years. Tom and his "sister" could never fathom why it was that she was never welcome at The Poplars.

That was by no means the end of the explaining she had to do. She decided to come a bit cleaner with James. She had indeed been a bit off colour when she rang him but that had been overtaken by events. Her mother had told her when in Canada that Alex had hoped that Kate would look after Alex's new-born baby and of course she was willing but it had come as a shock to her to have the child delivered so soon. She had been running around like a blue-arsed fly ever since but the problem seemed to be sorted now. She had found a very good live-in nanny so perhaps normality could be restored. She would be back at work as usual on Monday.

She now had to tackle a more difficult problem.

The most serious obstacle she had to face was "legitimising" her parenthood. According to the tale told to James, the baby was born in Canada but the last thing Kate wanted was a problem with the immigration authorities, which was quite likely to arise at some point in the future. Sooner or later, the need for a birth certificate would arise. Its absence would promote questions the answers to which might lead to disclosure of the truth. This had to be avoided at all costs. She made an appointment to attend the local Registry Office on the Thursday of the following week.

CHAPTER FOUR

Much against his will, Andrew Blake became a party to the conspiracy.

Kate made one last visit to Dubai. James had been scheduled to go but was more than happy to be replaced. Kate explained that she had some personal business to attend to. She took the next available flight to Dubai arriving late evening at the airport.

This time, there was no high-powered delegation to meet her. Presumably the Paki bitch had better things to do. There was, however, the same Range Rover driven by the same chauffeur. He had been expecting James but seemed pleased to see Kate and to take her to her hotel. Some things did not change.

At the hotel, she went straight to her room, showered, changed her clothes and went to the restaurant for a solitary, light, dinner, a marked contrast with her first visit there. After dinner, she returned to her room, took a double dose of the cold cure and slept soundly. She awoke to her alarm the following morning, showered, dressed, ate breakfast in her room and headed off to what promised to be a difficult encounter with her ex-husband.

The Range Rover dropped her off at Blake Construction. She presented herself to Andrew's secretary and was invited to take a seat. She took it for ten minutes; he was apparently making some sort of point. After the ten minutes, the Paki bitch emerged, silent and unsmiling and passed through the office without so much as a glance at Kate. After a further five minutes, the phone buzzed and Andrew's secretary informed her "Mr. Blake will see you now."

Andrew sat at his desk. He initially said nothing, merely holding out a hand in a gesture inviting Kate to take the chair at the opposite side of the desk. Then and only then did he speak:

"To what do I owe the honour of your visit? I was expecting James."

"Hello Andrew. Yes, I know you were but we have some private business to attend to."

"And what might that be?" he asked.

She had thought about this long and hard. She had gone over it time and time again on the plane. She was clear on the objective. She had to persuade Andrew to acknowledge the baby as his child. It was not going to be easy. She had decided that a direct, frontal, attack was the best option.

"Your daughter," she said, simply.

As expected, his initial reaction was puzzlement.

"What do you mean, 'my daughter'?"

"You have a daughter. She's in Birmingham right now being looked after by a nanny."

"How come this is the first I've heard? It's well over a year since we last had sex. She can't be mine."

"No, actually; she's not mine either."

Andrew was now totally confused.

Crunch point – the next revelation might ruin her life:

"I abducted her."

It took Andrew some seconds to take this in. He stared at her, muttered "What the...", sat bemused for several seconds more, then:

"Are you serious?"

"Very."

"That business in Birmingham, last week. That was you?" he asked, incredulous.

"Yes."

He paused again, took a deep breath. "You must be mad."

"You may be right. At least I might have been mad for a few seconds. But there it is. I have abducted a child."

A short silence ensued. Then Andrew spoke again. "Why have you come all this way to tell me this? What has it to do with me?"

"Because unless we get it right it could ruin us."

"What do you mean 'us'? What has it to do with me? Take my advice – get straight back to Birmingham and hand the child back."

"I can't do that. That would ruin us too."

"There's that 'us' again. Why should it bother me?"

"Just think about it. If we don't handle this

properly, I'll be finished… "

Andrew interrupted "You should have thought of that."

"I wish I had but I didn't think of anything. It was a moment's impulse. But we are where we are. As I say, unless we get it right – and I mean WE – I'll be ruined. Even if I hand the child back, I'll still be prosecuted and end up in prison. My returning the child might mitigate the sentence but two years instead of five would still be ruinous."

"Well it's got nothing to do with me…"

"Sorry, but it has."

"What do you mean?"

"Have you thought about the consequences of my going to prison? What happens to Tom?"

He had not thought about this. The possible consequences began to dawn on him. She continued:

"There are only two possibilities. Either he's brought up in care…"

"That's unthinkable."

"Or you take care of him. You and, I presume, the Paki bitch."

"I wish you'd stop calling her that. Her name's Sally."

"OK, that Sally bitch."

Andrew got angry. "You're the fucking bitch."

"May be. But what about Tom?"

"I couldn't possibly have him here. It's not just Sally – and I can't see her taking on your son – it's schools, everything. You know I never wanted children."

"So what's your solution?" Then she waxed more sympathetic, coaxing. "Think of this. Think of the child. She's really very lucky. She's going to get the best upbringing possible. Her family are probably scroungers from some council estate with five kids already. What sort of a future do you think she would have with them?"

"You've no idea who her family is. You're just trying to justify what you did."

"No, I can't justify it; I know that. But as I say, we are where we are. What do we do now?"

This time, he did not object to the "we". He was at a loss for words as he pondered his options:

"Look, I didn't ask for this. You're the one who did it. You've put me in a hell off a position."

Kate realised that she had won.

"You don't have to be implicated, you know. Just acknowledge that the child is yours. Why should you not be the father? We were married, we already have one child. Nobody but us keeps a diary of where and when we last fucked."

"So what do you want me to do?"

"All it will take is a flying visit to Birmingham, a short trip to the Registry Office to sign the register and you can fly back to Dubai and forget all about it. If there were ever any questions, you have all the answers. You had no idea about the abduction.

Naturally, you just took my word for it that she was your daughter."

Another long pause… "I don't know…"

"What else can we do? I know I shouldn't have done it. I was at a real low and there it was, in the pram. A momentary impulse is all it was. Do I regret it, yes," (a lie) "but it's done."

Andrew, silent, sighed again, but he was now a part of the "we". Eventually he asked, manifestly reluctant, "OK. What do we do?"

"I've made an appointment at the Registry Office for next Thursday. You fly over on the Wednesday, we do the business – I'm its mother, you're its father – then you fly back and forget all bout it."

"What do I tell Sally?"

"Nothing much. Tell her I've had a baby. I met this bloke flying back from Dubai. We got drunk on the plane and spent the night together in a Hotel at Heathrow… voila, a baby! You're doing the decent thing and acknowledging that it's yours."

All that remained were the details. Kate would see to that and let him know.

"See you on Wednesday, then, in Birmingham."

Andrew said nothing. She got up and left. Andrew called in his secretary and instructed her to book flights.

Sally had been very puzzled by Kate's flying

visit. Andrew had said nothing about it. It did not concern the business, he told her. It had to be some sort of private matter. In bed that night, after they had fucked and he had turned over to sleep, she taxed him with it.

"What did the ex-Mrs. Blake want?"

"What?" asked Andrew.

"Today, Kate was over, wasn't she? I wondered why."

"Nothing to concern you."

That seemed rather dismissive. Sally did not like it; was not satisfied. After a pause, she returned to the subject:

"But it does concern me. I'm not just some toy that you can pick up and play with whenever you feel like it. If there's still something going on between you two, I have a right to know about it."

"Ok, then, if you must know, she's had a baby. A daughter, and she says it's mine."

"And is it?"

"I don't know."

"What do you mean, you don't know. Can it be yours? Did you go on shagging her after you two split? How do you think that makes me feel? Did you? I can't believe that you did."

"No, we were never together again after that time when we broke up. You were there."

"So it's not yours then."

Andrew thought long and hard. He didn't want

56

Sally to know what it was all about but he realised that there might come a time in the future when it would be better if he had told her. He swore her to secrecy, got her to undertake never to breathe a word to anyone and told her the whole story.

"You're mad," she said. "This could well come back to bite you... us."

"So what's your suggestion, then? Bring Tom over here and look after him."

"Christ, no!"

That clinched it for Sally as it had for Andrew.

CHAPTER FIVE

The police had precious little to go on. A woman in a camel coat had emerged from the pharmacy next door, picked up the baby outside the corner shop, gone round the corner, placed the baby in the footwell of the passenger seat of a silver Audi A7 and driven off and the only evidence of any of this was that of a child, not yet three years old, who had seen a nice lady pick up the baby and take it round the corner and that of a woman who appeared to be one of the least observant witnesses ever to walk the earth.

Karen Ferguson, accompanied by a woman police constable trained for such situations, had had eventually to wheel the empty pram home with Seamus and break the news to Sean.

"Sonya's been taken," she almost screamed as she sobbed.

Sean was, as you would expect, initially incredulous, then stunned.

"What?... What th... "

The police constable intervened:

"I'm afraid your baby has been abducted. We don't know much about it yet but we are on the case. If she can be found, we'll find her."

The P.C. then made tea. They sat, silent but for the sound of sobs, trying to take it in. Karen took it particularly badly: they had lost Mollie; they had lost another pregnancy to a miscarriage. Eventually they had succeeded in establishing a family – two children – only, now, to have one of them snatched away. It hardly seemed possible.

The PC did what she could to comfort and settle them, but that was an unattainable objective and eventually she had to leave. She assured them that it was an extremely important case for her colleagues; they would take it very seriously; pursue their enquiries relentlessly and report regularly on progress. But Karen and Sean could not see what progress could be made.

Sean fed Seamus and knocked up bacon, eggs and fried bread for supper but Karen could not eat it. They switched the television set on and watched the report of the abduction of a baby from its pram on Powell Street. The police were pursuing their enquiries. Eventually, well after midnight and emotionally exhausted, they went to bed, but Karen did not sleep. In the course of the next day, they were asked to participate with the police in a press conference dealing with the abduction. Karen agreed and duly attended. She had nothing to say except that she loved their child and pleaded for Sonya's return, and she could not help but do it tearfully.

Sean refused to participate. Observing previous such press conferences had left him with the view that they were just a useless piece of "car-crash" television and he wanted nothing to do with it. He could not be persuaded otherwise.

For a while this prompted a suspicion that somehow, for some inexplicable reason, he was responsible for the disappearance of his own daughter. Perhaps there had been child abuse at home; perhaps, even, the baby had been killed and the abduction was a charade. But there was no doubting Seamus's evidence that "a nice lady had taken the baby". There was no way the child could have been coached to offer such convincing testimony. And in any case, such a plot ran the serious risk of negative evidence. There would almost certainly have been people around the whole time who would be able to state categorically that no abduction had taken place.

Once that speculative line of enquiry was abandoned, the police had nothing left. There were the usual appeals for witnesses to come forward but nothing came of any of it. The case was never dropped but it was allowed to stagnate, and it stagnated for years.

It did not stagnate for Karen and Sean but it did succeed in ruining their lives. After several months during which no progress in solving the crime was made Sean became more and more accepting of the view that the child had been taken and murdered. He had persuaded Karen that they should ask the police about such a possible outcome. Karen would never accept it and felt vindicated when the detective in charge expressed the commonly held view that abductions conducted by women rarely resulted in the death of the child. More often than not, the child would be restored to its parents. Women abductors were usually mentally ill and incapable of maintaining a pretence for long.

With men, it was wholly different. Abduction and murder of a small child commonly accompanied a particular type of male perversion.

The breach slowly developed.

"You have to accept it," insisted Sean to Karen. "Sonya's dead. We'd have heard something by now. We have to move on."

"Don't say that… ever. She's not dead. She's out there somewhere. We just have to find her."

What Sean came rightly to regard as Karen's obsession eventually made life together, in his view, impossible and Karen appeared not to care whether it was possible or not. The financial implications of her giving up her job were just a small part of it. Karen would go off, walking mile after mile, in the desperate hope of finding Sonya and she blamed Sean for not joining in the search. Most unforgivable of all, to Sean, was that she seemed almost to forget Seamus's existence.

Sean would get home after work to find that Seamus had not been fed all day. On one occasion, Seamus had been in the house alone, goodness knows for how long, when Sean arrived back from work. When Seamus started attending nursery school, Karen had greater liberty to pursue her quest and went farther and farther afield, frequently failing to collect Seamus from school, either because she had forgotten or because she had put herself out of reach. Constant calls from the school to Sean's place of work and his consequent necessary early departures began to have an impact on his job as well as his married life.

Logically, you might have thought, things would be at their worst at the start, gradually, perhaps almost imperceptibly, getting better, but the opposite seemed to be the case with Karen.

Eventually, the break in the marriage came. It had to come. One of the casualties had been their sex life and Sean had been prepared to live with that. He understood. And he did not break faith with Karen. But there came a point where he finally admitted to himself that he deserved a better life and demanded of Karen that she abandon her quest.

When she refused, he left. To be strictly accurate, the outcome of the final tearful row was that Karen left, taking Seamus, to live with her mother while Sean continued to live at the house. Taking in lodgers enabled him to live and pay a modest weekly sum by way of maintenance of Karen and Seamus, but the break was clear and final.

Eventually, they were divorced. Sean managed to restart his life. He met a young widow, Vicky, through work – changing her tyres morphed into changing their lives. They went out a few times; all went well. Eventually she went to live at the house – her job solved the money problems. In course of time, they married and so far as Sean was concerned, Karen was relegated to history along with their daughter. Seamus was not. Karen's full-time preoccupation with her lost daughter left her with little time for Seamus. And his grandmother, never happy even with her role as part-time carer now found the role of full-time carer thrust upon her. She refused to accept it. Sean was more than happy to have his son back and from then on Seamus lived with his father, then with him and Vicky and finally as a member of their new, extended, family.

Karen never reconciled herself to the idea of Sonya's disappearance. She never reached Sean's state of resigned acceptance. She never allowed that Sonya was dead; she continued her eternal search. She never worked again. Her mother now had to assume Sean's role as the subject of her dogmatic insistence on Sonya's survival and if a mother could have divorced a child, she would very probably have done so.

Sonya's abduction ruined lives. Kate's conduct, measured in terms of its consequences, amounted to more than murder.

CHAPTER SIX

George

At school, George excelled at nothing; nothing licit, that is. So far as his academic studies were concerned, he did as little as he could get away with and despite the best efforts of tutors, failed to reach the mediocre. Nor was he blessed with the talents, physical and mental, which might have allowed him to make some sort of mark in athletic activities. It was not a case of excelling; rather of reaching a standard which ensured that you were not picked last when teams were selected.

He did learn some things. He first learned how to masturbate. Then he learned how to smoke cigarettes, then how to obtain cigarettes to smoke. Later, he learned how to smoke cannabis. That was obtainable from a sixth-former, Coulthard, two years ahead of George. Nobody knew where Coulthard got it from until he was about to leave, at which point he passed on the secrets of his trade to George, one of the few who could afford to purchase them.

It was quite simple. On the chosen day and at the chosen time the exchange would take place just inside the wood, which flanked the school cricket pitch. Each week, the varied chosen day and time would be set for the following week. It was impossible for the school to police. Cricket balls (or, in winter, hockey balls) were hit into the wood dozens of times a day and somebody had to recover them. This was one thing that George was very good at but, sadly, not quite good enough.

It was strictly cash on delivery but George always had cash. Obtaining the goods was just one benefit, which accrued from this exchange. Through it, George became acquainted with a minor and fringe aspect of the local underworld, itself not the greatest criminal enterprise ever known to mankind. But it meant that, when he had to leave school, George had an entrée into the life, which he led, with a few varied interruptions, for most of the following twenty years.

It was not inevitable that the school's chief cannabis dealer would eventually be caught and expelled; Coulthard had avoided it. George did not. The school was well aware that the weed was available on school premises. Dog-ends in the dormitory and the smell alone were sufficient evidence. The staff kept a casual eye on things and when George was spotted emerging from the wood not only with a cricket ball but also with a mysterious package, the game was up.

Rosalie was duly notified and headed off immediately to the school to plead with the Head for another chance for her wayward son but in vain. Had there been anything on the credit side of his ledger, a second chance might have been possible – the school did not readily forgo its fees - but there was not.

Rosalie waited while George packed his things and carried them out to the BMW. Rosalie spoke not a word until they were out of the school gates and on their way back to Burton. Once on the road, however, she gave him a very large piece of her mind:

"Have you any idea how much I've spent on your education at that place?" (A bit unkind, this; a few tens of thousands made hardly any dint at all in the Forester millions under her control.)

George had little idea but said nothing.

"Tens of thousands of pounds, and for what?"

"So what?" asked George. "You can afford it. And in any case, it was your decision, your choice. I never wanted to go to that fucking school anyway."

"Watch your language. You're not with your junkie mates now."

A stony silence occupied the next fifteen minutes of the journey, then Rosalie started again:

"Well, what are you thinking of doing with your life now? You're sixteen; you've got no qualifications – at all. What can you do?"

"Oh, I'll think of something. Anyway, I don't need to work, do I? I can live well enough on my trust income."

"That's up to the trustees. You may find that their generosity has limits."

Perhaps it should have had, but it did not and George continued to receive his £25,000 per annum.

It would not keep him in luxury but it would ensure that he could meet the cost of necessities, as defined by him, even though Rosalie insisted that he pay for his board and lodgings at The Poplars.

Rosalie did not leave it there. She got in touch with her old contacts at Foresters' Brewery and they agreed, for old times' sake, to take George on in an unskilled capacity. Rosalie nagged him into accepting. It was never going to last.

First a race meeting at Wrexham proved to be a more attractive prospect than heaving barrels in the yard at Foresters'. Then an irregular series of late nights at the Admiral Benbow (where, George had discovered, the barmaid was not unusually concerned about the age of her customers) resulting in late starts and absences produced the inevitable result.

Had George needed to earn in order to live, he might have made more of an effort (although that is doubtful), but he did not. In the event, he was more than happy to be dismissed. He did not miss his wages. They were minuscule by comparison with his unearned income. He settled into a life where the greater part of most days was spent with his newfound mates at the Admiral Benbow, playing darts and dominoes, scoffing hamburgers and drinking and smoking more than he actually enjoyed. It was what you did.

George soon discovered that the Admiral Benbow had other virtues. It offered a ready market for cannabis. He made contact with his old suppliers and established a small but profitable business there. It became more profitable when a territorial rival complained about his prices being undercut. George would have happily raised his without the emphasis of a bloody nose and some bruising which accompanied the request. It was all the same to him; he did not rely on the trade.

In due course, the range of goods offered expanded to embrace first heroin and then cocaine. George himself had the good sense to avoid the former but became a regular user of the latter via which he eventually gained access to more elevated social circles in and around Birmingham.

When he eventually received the capital from the trust he bought himself a Bentley Continental. This identified him as a person of consequence and not merely a supplier of cocaine. Bit by bit, his habits and his tastes changed and discovered what was destined ultimately to become his salvation - wine.

In these elevated social circles, he would also discover Val who eventually became his partner, through thick and thin, most of it, for several years during which she remained loyal, thin.

Years before these events, George had managed to find time to take driving lessons. Rosalie refused to encourage this although the thought did cross her mind that at least he was learning something. Shortly after his seventeenth birthday, he took and passed his driving test and immediately headed off to a local second-hand car dealer and bought himself a six-year old souped-up Ford Escort.

It was a lethal combination. With a mate in the passenger seat and a couple of birds in the back, George could not resist the temptation to demonstrate what a great driver he was and how fast his machine would go. Three speeding tickets in the space of as many months put his licence on the line. There was a familiar air of inevitability about it when the Escort left the road and ended up in a ditch and hedge. He was, in a sense, lucky. No-one in the car or elsewhere was seriously injured otherwise some form of detention would have been inevitable.

The resulting dangerous driving conviction cost him his licence and a four hundred and twenty pound fine. He could easily afford this but worse was to come.

The disqualification did not stop George driving. It was too inconvenient. It did not stop him speeding either. That would have robbed him of the excitement. When the police car behind flashed its light and signalled him to stop, late one Saturday night, George had the good sense not to pull over. At least, it seemed like good sense at the time; accompanying him and his friends in the car was an amount of cocaine, which could only have been for his own use if he had been able to live to be a hundred years old.

69

There was something ineffable about George's turning madly into a cul-de-sac in order to escape. Charges of driving whilst disqualified and dangerous driving would themselves have probably ensured a stay in a young offenders' institution. Dealing in illegal substances guaranteed it and George spent two years in what had at one time been a Borstal institution not far from The Poplars.

The proximity did not ensure frequent visits from his mother. Her main contribution to attempts at rehabilitation consisted of her getting rid of his car. At the end of his detention, she allowed him to return to The Poplars – he had nowhere else to go – but only reluctantly. His return hardly made any difference to his behaviour. He resumed his former life in the town. If he returned to The Poplars to sleep, it was usually in the early hours of the morning. Frequently, he did not return at all.

Rosalie soon gave up cooking breakfast. She saw little of her son but, to be honest, she did not want to see more of him. She had nothing to communicate to him but resentment. He said nothing to her; if he did, it prompted nothing but hostility.

The resumption of George's freedom may have made little impact on his lifestyle but it did on Rosalie's. Of course, no-one blamed her for her son's misdemeanours. How could they be her responsibility? Nevertheless, they were elephants in the room at coffee mornings. Even at the bridge table, where silence was welcome, they make a significant difference to her social life.

Bit by bit, fewer of her invitations were accepted. The invitations of others to her fell away. She was eventually reduced to very few friends who were, though Rosalie was reluctant to admit it, flattered by her wealth. For Rosalie, it was bad enough that her son had turned out as he had. It was even worse that it should have had such a damaging effect on her own social life. A lonely widow, that was all the life she had and that remained the case for the rest of her days.

George lacked the sense to find a distribution point other than the Admiral Benbow and it was inevitable that he would again be arrested, charged, convicted and, this time, having reached formal adulthood, sentenced to three years in prison. His mother visited him but once. That was in order to inform him that The Poplars was no longer his home. When released, he would have to live elsewhere. She blamed him, with considerable justification, for her isolation. She wanted nothing further to do with him.

George left prison after two years – the only instance of "good behaviour" ever recorded in the first few decades of his life. He did not bother to try to return to The Poplars. He was just as keen as his mother that he should stay away, for good, and he did so. He spent a few weeks in a girlfriend's flat and then rented a larger one for himself. She moved in with him and his life moved on from there.

CHAPTER SEVEN

Andrew Blake duly arrived at Birmingham airport on the Wednesday as arranged. His secretary had been unable to book a seat on a scheduled flight to Birmingham and he had had to fork out for a seat on a private jet. That had made his bad mood worse.

His secretary had arranged for him to stay the night at the Royal Plaza. Kate did not want him at her place. Sally would have exploded had that been the plan. Anyway, a night in a hotel was, to Andrew's way of thinking, preferable to spending twenty-four hours in Kate's company.

Whilst the Royal Plaza would have suited ninety per cent of mankind perfectly well, Andrew reminded himself that he was accustomed to something better and made a mental note to register his dissatisfaction with his secretary on his return.

Kate had arranged for her and Andrew to have breakfast together at the hotel in order to make sure that he was fully briefed about his role. He had assumed thus far that this would consist of little more than being present, summoning a smile and signing his name. He was distinctly unhappy when Kate spelled it out for him:

"Right. Here's how it is. I was caught short; there was no time to get me to hospital. I had the baby on the bathroom floor; you were present."

"Hang on. What's all this about? I thought I

just had to turn up and say I was the father."

"Yes, but also, they will require proof of birth – the usual thing is a letter from a hospital or maternity home, as I understand it. Even a letter or something from a midwife if it is a home birth, I assume. We have none of these so unless you know a midwife who is inclined to perjury this is the only way we can overcome the hurdle."

"So I have to say I assisted you at the birth, do I? If they ask, I haven't a clue apart from the fact that the brat emerges from your cunt."

"Christ, you disgust me. But, no, you don't have to say that you helped... just that you were there. My sister, Alex, who was, as you know, a doctor, happened to be visiting and she did the necessary."

"Ok, fair enough. I just stood and watched, is that what you want?"

"Exactly."

"What's with the 'was a doctor'? Has she been struck off or something?"

"Christ, don't you remember? She died – of cancer – in Canada."

"No I didn't know; you never told me."

"Oh, forget it. Have you got it straight now? You were there, you observed me giving birth. Alex attended me. It's not rocket science."

"OK, let's go and get it over with. Remember, I genuinely believe it's my child, our child. I know

74

nothing about your fucking abducting a baby."

"Absolutely. That's not going to arise and even if it did, you're in the clear. We were married. We have one child. We now have another. You have no reason to doubt that it's yours, OK?"

With that, they headed off to the Registry. When they gave their account of "the birth" there was some hesitation although not so much as to prompt a raised eyebrow. When asked if Dr. Alex Forester could certify the birth, they explained that she had returned to Canada. And when pressed further, having to "reveal" that she had died, eyebrows did twitch. Kate explained that the purpose of her sister's visit was to say a final farewell to family and friends. There was some discussion with another registrar and the deed was done. Sarah Jane Blake came officially into being. The formalities were soon concluded. Kate and Andrew left.

As soon as they were clear, Andrew exploded. "You didn't tell me it would have my name," he shouted.

"Oh, come on. What the fuck did you expect? You're the father. What did you think its father was going to be called? 'Santa Claus'?"

"Stony" was altogether too nuanced an adjective to describe the silence that surrounded their drive back to the airport. The fact that he had four hours to wait for a flight, and that only to Schiphol where he had another two hour wait, did not improve Andrew's mood. Kate had got what she wanted – and needed. She had nothing more to say to her ex-husband. She dropped him off without a word, not even a mumbled 'thanks'. Nor did he have anything to say. His mind was still wrestling with the notion that something might go wrong but the deed was done. He had to live with it.

CHAPTER EIGHT

It would be a mistake to say that the police were continuing their investigation into the abduction of Sonya Ferguson. There was nothing to continue. They had had little enough to go on in the first place and no new leads had emerged. Only one person concerned cared nothing as to whether there was any progress or not. That was Sonya herself.

Sonya had, of course, disappeared not only in person but also in name. She had become, officially, Sarah Jane Blake and was living, well-cared for and very comfortably, with her new mother, Kate Forester and her new nanny Vittoria.

From the start, Kate had dropped the "Blake". She had resumed her maiden name after the divorce and now bestowed it, for all purposes, on her new daughter. There was nothing strange about this. Whichever version of events you had been schooled in it caused no problems. Alex's "daughter" was, naturally, a Forester. Alex had never married (and was now beyond the libel, if such it was, of having been said to have given birth to a bastard child). And as far as the rest were concerned bestowing upon the daughter of a dissolved marriage the maiden name of her mother was commonplace, whatever the birth certificate said.

Tom, by this time three years old was, now, also a Forester at least in the eyes of all in the world outside Dubai. And they did not care what the children were called.

As far as Tom was concerned, he had a new baby sister and her name, he quickly learned, was Sarah. And in so far as it makes any sense to attribute such an emotion to a three-year old, he loved his new sister from the start. At home, he wanted always to be in her company, sometimes to the point of inconvenience. He got in the way at bath-time and complained every night at being put to bed in a different room. When he started nursery school and had to leave her behind every week-day he cried and was never properly reconciled until he returned home. When, three years later, Sarah was enrolled at the same nursery school, normality was, in Tom's eyes, restored for the time being.

For the rest of the household things settled down into a pleasurable routine. Vittoria was delighted to have both a baby daughter in her care and a three-year old son. This in turn enabled Kate to feel contented and, gradually, more secure. She returned to work with a renewed enthusiasm, each day more and more assured about the regime, which now prevailed in her extended ménage.

The only cloud on her horizon was her mother, Rosalie. Kate never reached the point of expecting that Rosalie would come to accept Sarah as a granddaughter but she had hoped that some sort of an amicable relationship might emerge and although

Rosalie eventually came to acknowledge Sarah as some sort of friend of Tom, Kate's hopes remained always frustrated until ultimately they were eroded by Rosalie's immutable refusal to acknowledge Sarah's place in the family.

Kate may effectively have lost one associate member of her household but she unexpectedly gained another.

She was aware that Vittoria had a regular visitor. She had made it as clear as possible at the start that Vittoria was to regard her rooms as home and no problems had arisen - no wild parties, no strange young men staying overnight.

On the first occasion when she encountered her, Kate was introduced by Vittoria to Isabella, thereafter always "Bella". Bella was also Portuguese. She was a trained chef but had so far failed to find a job, which offered her charge of her own kitchen. Some weeks after the first meeting between Kate and Bella Vittoria asked if she could have a word with Kate.

"Of course. What is it? I hope to God you're not going to tell me you want to leave. Should I be paying you more?" All this before Vittoria had a chance to speak. Eventually she managed:

"No, no, it's nothing like that. I'm more than happy with my job here. No, it's about Bella." She hesitated. Kate nudged her:

"Yes?"

"I don't know how you feel about these things… but… well, Bella and I are in love. We're partners."

Kate had had no inkling about this but immediately admitted to herself that she must have been blind. It had been common enough at school so why should it not happen in the adult outside world.

"Oh, that's lovely for you. I'm very happy for you," she said, and waited.

Vittoria eventually summoned up the determination. "I was wondering if it might be possible for her to come and live here with me. In my rooms, I mean. We wouldn't bother you… "

"Of course, why not?" interrupted Kate. Then she asked, with nothing particular in mind, "What does she do? I presume she would want to carry on working. Is living here convenient for her?"

"Actually, she's a trained chef but she has to work as a kitchen skivvy. Nobody so far is prepared to put her in charge of a kitchen. It's a waste. It's a pity because she's actually very good."

It was a spur-of-the-moment thing but Kate never regretted it.

"I don't suppose she would be prepared to work here, as a chef, I mean – well, what am I saying – as a cook?" The Forester fortune could afford it.

"Oh, we hadn't thought about anything like that; but I'll ask her, shall I?"

She did ask. The answer was an enthusiastic

"Yes". Bella joined the household and the cuisine improved immensely. It had never been Kate's strong point and dinner was frequently something picked up at a takeaway on her way home. Beyond feeding babies, Vittoria had hardly any pretensions of a culinary sort whatsoever.

One consequence of this was that Tom grew up in a household of females. It had an effect on the development of his personality. He often felt, in his later life, that he had never learned to be at ease in the company of men though it never bothered him. Throughout his childhood and his adolescence he had never wanted anyone's company other than Sarah's.

Who knows where love comes from? We normally associate it with sex. The female's display presents her with choice and she selects the male with the greatest appeal – then something deeply puzzlingly psychological happens. Not so with Tom and Sarah. They were in love long before they had any notion of what sex was about. From the earliest days, one would sneak into the other's bedroom and they would spend the night together despite efforts, unenthusiastic if the truth be told, by Kate and Vittoria to discourage the practice.

In the same fashion, they came to know one another's bodies. At first they would bathe together and later never experienced any discomfort in sharing a bathroom. There was nothing overtly sexual about any of this. They would have been perplexed if anyone had suggested that there might be.

When Tom reached eight years of age, his attendance at a local independent preparatory school for boys presented another crisis. This time, it was not abated. When her turn came, Sarah was enrolled at the girls' school. These daily separations were, however, tolerable. Each knew that at the end of the day they would be reunited. That came to an end when the time came for Tom to go away to school. George's experience at The Birches ruled that school out and Tom ended up in St. Illtyd's, a decent enough school just over the border in Wales. For three years, Sarah saw Tom only on occasional weekends and during vacations. When she, in her turn, went to Jevington, their time spent together dwindled even further.

The character of their occasional meetings, however, changed. Tom's departure for St. Illtyd's coincided with puberty and at that school he learned about sex. What he gleaned and how he gleaned it would not find a place in any reputable text on sex education. The idea of love, of being in love with someone, never entered into it. His experience of sex started with masturbation and passed through a phase of mutual masturbation with school-friends before Tom ever turned his mind to the idea of finding sexual satisfaction with a member of the opposite sex.

Sarah's experience at Jevington was very

similar. What happened to them during Sarah's first long vacation from Jevington took them both by surprise.

Although Kate and Vittoria took the matter of sleeping arrangements more seriously as Tom and Sarah grew up, they still contrived to sleep together when they were both at home. They had always held one another and snuggled and kissed but now they encountered a further phase. Tom had previously, occasionally, experienced an erection when tucked up with Sarah and this improbable development had been the cause of some amusement between them. Now, when the phenomenon recurred, Tom first explained then demonstrated that he could ejaculate. Sarah observed it, puzzled and fascinated. She moved on from there to doing it for him, a wholly different and much more pleasurable experience for Tom, in no wise impaired by Sarah's giggling which accompanied her efforts.

Much later Sarah developed breasts and pubic hair. They inevitably came into play. She enjoyed fondling her breasts. Even more, she enjoyed Tom caressing her. Sarah also enjoyed exploring her pubic area, even more so when Tom learned to do as he was told.

It was inevitable that they should eventually have sex. It occurred on a summer break at the *manoir* near Pont-Farcy. The household had settled into the habit of always spending some weeks there in the summer. The standard pattern was for Tom, Sarah and Vittoria to be permanent residents for this time and for others, chiefly Kate and Bella to join them for spells of three or four days, usually long week-ends. After some years of refusal, Rosalie even condescended to spend a little time with her family in France, her family plus, of course, Tom's friend Sarah (or was it Sonya, she would perplex herself by asking herself.)

The permanent trio of Sarah, Tom and Vittoria might visit the beach or go for country walks. They might just idle around the swimming pool. On such occasions, there was little need for Vittoria to act as a chaperone. It was back at the house, especially during the nights, when she perhaps should have discharged such a function more efficiently but she did not do so. The reality of it was that, as Vittoria recognised, they truly loved one another and it seemed to her to be a beautiful thing rather than an offence against one of Man's more stupid laws.

Of course, it became more problematic when Sarah reached puberty. When their practices nevertheless continued, Vittoria admitted to herself that the time had come for her to intervene but she did so half-heartedly and, in consequence, ineffectually.

What had to happen eventually did happen. They had been to the beach and on returning back to the house, Vittoria had retired to the kitchen to set about preparing an evening meal. Sarah and Tom went upstairs to shower away the sand and change for the evening. They showered together, as they frequently did, but on this occasion, drying one another down morphed into caressing. Her breasts and his penis were well dry before they retired to Sarah's room, still laughing, although they both knew what they were about to do.

They were still naked. They were kissing. Tom was tenderly touching Sarah's breasts and she was fondling his penis. Surprisingly, it was Sarah who took the initiative:

"Can we try fucking? Lots of the girls at school say they've done it; I don't know whether to believe them or not. But we've never done it; I'd really like to feel what it's like."

So they did. It was at first an exploratory partly-painful, stop-and-start, business but it culminated in an unexpected and unprecedented pleasure for both.

They continued to make love for at least two more years, though not without encountering some very serious obstacles on the way. They were, after all, brother and sister, were they not, and they came to know that the fruit they were enjoying was forbidden and that knowledge inhibited their behaviour only to the extent that they accepted that it was necessary to be cautious in order to avoid discovery. It in no way affected their behaviour or their attitude to on another. The simply thought that such a categorisation of their relationship was wrong and unfair.

It was Bella who actually caught them at it, one afternoon after returning unexpectedly early from the shops. She was shocked but it was not her part to remonstrate. She immediately reported it to Vittoria who was obliged to insist that they desist. As soon as Kate returned from work that day, Vittoria reported the events to her. Tom and Sarah were immediately summoned for a confrontation with Kate and Vittoria. Kate had by now firmly fixed Sarah In her mind as her daughter. She launched straight in:

"Don't you two know what you've been doing is awful? You're brother and sister. You can't do that. It's immoral – it's illegal. Have you never heard of 'incest'? Brother and sister can't have sex together. This has to cease, immediately and forever. Do you hear what I say?"

Kate and Tom looked at each other. They could not accept this. They loved one another purely and innocently. What they were doing could not be wrong. It felt so right. Tom expostulated: "But we love each other". Sarah nodded vigorously. "When we are older…"

Kate intervened. "That's another thing. You're both much too young to be doing this."

Tom continued "When we are old enough, we shall get married, shan't we Sarah?"

Sarah had not previously thought in these terms but immediately voiced her assent:

"Yes, we shall."

"No you won't. You can't. Don't you understand? Do you hear what I am saying? Brother and sister can't get married. It's against the law. This stops NOW, and forever. Is that clear? If I have to, I shall lock you in your rooms at night. IS THAT CLEAR?"

Well, it was clear. At least, to Tom and Sarah, it was clear what their mother thought about it, even if they were as far from agreeing with her, as it was possible to be. There was nothing to say but "yes". Both muttered assent. Neither intended that the clarity was going to bring any change in their relationship although both could see that it was going to make it more problematic.

Vittoria had sat silently throughout the whole of this confrontation. She agreed with everything that Kate had had to say and, looking at the pair of them, had nodded assent from time to time. But she saw something that Kate missed. Kate's admonitions were going to have little effect on their behaviour other than to make things more difficult for Tom and Sarah. They were going to have to make sure that they were not caught again. They were not going to shake hands and say, "It's been nice knowing you."

At the first opportunity, which presented itself, Vittoria took Sarah aside:

"About what your mother said," she began.

"You should do as she says. You're heading for trouble if you don't" but she continued:

"All the same, it's time you started to take precautions. You know what I mean?"

Sarah clearly did not. Vittoria went on "You realise you're running the risk of having a baby, don't you?"

Sarah nodded although, to be honest, it was not something, which occupied the forefront of their minds.

"Well you should take precautions. Don't ever tell your mother that I said this, but there's a pill you should take to make sure you can't get pregnant and whenever, if ever, you have sex with a boy, or a man, you should insist that he wears a condom, at least until you are happily married and want to have babies."

Vittoria embarked on the necessary explanation. "That's a rubbery sheath the man puts on his penis so that he can't make you pregnant. Do you understand?"

Sarah partially understood. With Vittoria's help, her advice was duly implemented - most of the time. At least one risk had been largely eliminated, not, however, as events were to establish, entirely.

CHAPTER NINE

Tom's progress at St. Illtyd's would have satisfied all but the most demanding of parents. He twice won the school prize for his year and although he was too small to make an adequate impression on the rugby field, which, sadly, mattered most at a Welsh school, he made the first eleven at cricket.

When the time came, he managed two As and a B in his A-levels and found himself with a choice of places at university. He selected Warwick, not for any relevant, academic, reasons but because it would enable him to return home on the weekends when Sarah was back from Jevington.

"Home" was now his second home. Once he had settled on Warwick as his choice, Kate bought him a small one-bedroomed flat. He had taken his driving lessons and Kate also bought him a Renault Clio. The Forester fortune could afford it. From Kate's point of view, it turned out to be a catastrophic error. Sarah, still only fifteen, ceased to be satisfied with occasional weekend meetings with Tom when a vastly more attractive alternative occurred to her.

Informing her mother took Kate completely by surprise:

"I'm leaving school."

"I beg your pardon," exclaimed Kate, incredulous.

"I said I'm leaving school."

"What on earth are you talking about? You're still only fifteen. You can't leave until the end of the year. In any case, what about your A-levels? You've got to do the sixth form before you leave."

"I'll do them somewhere else. I've had enough of Jevington."

"So what are you proposing to do? Live here and go to the local comprehensive?" For Kate, such a course was lunatic. The local school was alright – good enough for the local hoi polloi that is. But hardly for a Forester.

"I'm not going to live here. I'm going to move in with Tom in Warwick."

For Kate, this was an appalling proposition from all points of view:

"You certainly are not! It's an absurd idea. I absolutely will not allow it, do you understand?"

"How are you proposing to stop me? Lock me in my room here; chain me to the furniture in Jevington?"

"Don't be ridiculous. You're staying at Jevington until you've done you're A-levels. That's that!"

But of course that was not that. Kate even threatened to call in the Attendance Officer but it made no difference to Sarah. The following weekend, when Kate went to Jevington to collect Sarah, she was not there. All her things had disappeared. Tom had beaten Kate to the punch and driven down to

Jevington in the Clio on the Friday afternoon. When Kate arrived at the school, they were already unpacking the car in Warwick.

As soon as she understood what had happened, Kate drove immediately to Tom's flat in Warwick. She rang the bell. Tom appeared at the door and, seeing that it was his mother, opened it wide to let her in. Kate launched her attack immediately, in the hall:

"I assume Sarah's here. I've come to collect her. She's going back to Jevington."

Tom said nothing. He opened the door and ushered his mother into the sitting room of the flat. There sat Sarah.

"Pack your things – immediately. You're coming with me. You're going back to Jevington – today."

Tom was surprised at Sarah's boldness as, indeed, was she:

"No I'm not. I'm staying here with Tom."

"Do as I say. You're going back to finish your schooling at Jevington. Do as I say – NOW!"

Sarah did not move. She remained silent for a few moments then continued:

"I've told you. I'm staying here with Tom from now on. I shall never come home again."

"You're coming with me this instant," insisted Kate and reached down to grab Sarah by the arm. Sarah shook off her hand:

"You think you can make me?" she shouted. "How are you going to do it? Tie me up and bundle me in the boot? I'm not coming – you can't make me…"

Kate turned to Tom who had thus far remained silent:

"Tell her – you can't do this. I've explained. You'll get into no end of trouble if you do this."

Tom's silence continued.

In the end, Kate had no choice but to accept the fact until she could find some way of putting an end to what seemed to her like a disastrous state of affairs, as indeed it turned out to be – but not just for them.

She stomped her way to the door and left, slamming it behind her. She was angry, frustrated and afraid. She drove off with no idea what to do next.

Someone else did. Before Sarah joined him in Warwick, unknown to him, Tom had made quite an impression on Angela, a second-year student in the flat next door. When she learned, bit-by-bit, that he was not only good-looking and intelligent but also filthy-rich, she had mounted a determined campaign. She had started by "arranging" to bump into him as they both left the building and exchanging unnecessarily cheery greetings. She had contrived to walk into the university with him on a couple of occasions but the conversation had turned out to be stilted and one-sided. She had knocked on his door on one occasion and, when he opened it, asked him:

"I'm just going out to get a pizza. I wondered if you wanted one? Shall I get one for you?"

Tom had by now gleaned some idea of what was going on. He was not in the least interested in a pizza but he mustered a smile as he declined. Angela mistakenly registered this as encouragement.

The next evening, she made her big throw. She took off her day-time clothes and her bra and put on a button-fronted dress. She left undone the maximum number of buttons she dared to and went and knocked on Tom's door. He opened it.

"Sorry to bother you but have you got a microwave? Mine's stopped working."

Tom hesitated only briefly then, fully opening the door, said:

"No problem. Come on in."

She did not enter immediately. "Can I use your microwave?"

"Of course," Tom replied. He noticed that she seemed to have dressed somewhat casually but it did not excite his interest.

"I'll just go get my stuff," she said, went back to her flat and returned holding a couple of packages. "It'll take about ten minutes. Is that alright?"

"Of course. Come on in."

He ushered her into the kitchen, showed her the microwave and left her to it, returning to the sitting room and parking himself on the sofa. Within a few seconds, she joined him and sat down on the sofa next to hm. Crossing her legs revealed a great deal of thigh and her leaning towards him to thank him revealed a great deal of breast. He merely registered this and remained unaffected by it. He did not fancy her at all. He fancied only Sarah.

Angela asked him a few questions, how was the work going? Did he get home often? Where was home? As she did so, she re-crossed her legs and pressed a thigh against his. She turned to face him and made it obvious that a kiss, and whatever might ensue upon it, were welcome. His response was to change seats, moving to an armchair. She got the message and sat silently until the ping of the microwave signified that it was time for her to depart. She collected her meal, thanked him unsmilingly and went back to her room, angry, frustrated and humiliated.

Angela became aware of Sarah almost as soon as Sarah joined Tom. She was furious. "She's just a child," she said to herself. Her fury was much abated when Tom introduced Sarah as his sister. When, however, on that very same evening, sounds penetrated the party wall between her flat and Tom's the explanation offered by Tom became less convincing. Incredulous at first, she was ultimately obliged to conclude that the noise could only be that of two people having sex; and her fury was rekindled more fiercely than it had burned before.

The following day, it was Angela who called in at the Social Services Department and asked to speak to someone about "a situation, which I find disturbing." Ushered into an office and sitting opposite Alice Walker, a social worker, she continued:

"You may well think this is none of my business – I'm not sure I should be here – but I thought it was something you should know about and I can't see that raising it with you can do any harm."

"So what is this 'situation', Angela?" asked Alice and Angela set it out for her:

"I have a flat in Epsom Grove. I'm next door to a flat occupied by a chap called Tom Forester. His sister appears to have moved in with him. I met her yesterday. He's a first year student. She looks about fourteen."

"Ok, but nothing really odd about a brother and sister sharing a flat, is there?"

"Well..." Angela hesitated. It was a more-than-competent thespian performance. "I think they're having sex together."

"Ah! That would shed a different light, wouldn't it? Are you sure? How do you know?"

"This is what's so embarrassing about it. I'm not spying on them. I took what Tom said at face value. But they are one-bedroomed flats and the party wall between his flat and mine isn't exactly sound-proof" (she did not mention that she had had to stick her ear to the wall to be more sure) "and I couldn't help but hear them at it last night."

"Hear SOMEONE at it, perhaps, but have you any reason to suppose it was the little sister? Tom probably has a girlfriend. Isn't that a more likely explanation?"

Angela felt an idiot. She had not thought of that, thought, that is, of ruling out that possibility before going to the Social Services Department. She quickly recovered:

"That's possible, of course, but so far as I know, Tom doesn't have a girlfriend. And I don't think anybody visited them last night. The walls are thin, as I say, and you tend to hear if anyone is coming or going."

Alice became sceptical. Was there something slightly unsavoury about Angela's pursuit of her neighbours? Perceptively, she wondered if she was dealing with a woman scorned. She was reminded of elderly ladies peeping through the net curtains to keep an eye on the street:

"Right! Well, leave it with me. I'll think about it and if it looks as though we should enquire further, we will... But thanks for bringing it to our attention." She rose out of her chair. Angela took the hint:

"Well, thanks for seeing me. I hope there's nothing to it. I just thought I'd better..." and rose in her turn.

"Quite right. Good morning then."

"Good morning," replied Angela, and left.

Alice pondered the matter for a little while. She was inclined to go for the obvious explanation – Tom had a girlfriend. But it was a one-bedroomed flat. Where was the sister sleeping? She picked up the phone and called her opposite number in the police force and set out the situation for her. She had successfully passed the buck.

Police-sergeant Joanne Helby, in charge of child welfare, now faced the same dilemma as Alice Walker. But if it turned out that there was something to it and she had not bothered to do anything, the shit might hit the fan, quite possibly in a big way.

After they had endured the admonitions of their mother and Vittoria, Tom and Sarah had become aware that if their relationship was not to be prejudiced it was necessary for them to take care not to advertise it. So that when the doorbell rang that evening and, opening the door, they were confronted by a person introducing herself as "Police-sergeant Joanne Helby" they were immediately put on their guard.

They invited her in, sat her down in the armchair and, from the sofa, waited to hear what she had to say. What she had to say lacked the ring of truth:

"I'm sorry to bother you, but we've had complaints about excessive noise emanating from your flat," (which was, of course, true even if not in the sense in which she described it). It had not occurred to her to think that, there having been no noise to complain about, this would immediately put them on their guard, suspicious about the real purpose of her call.

"Not from this flat," Tom immediately insisted. "Who complained? What about, exactly?"

"I'm afraid I can't tell you that. We received the information in confidence." Then, after a pause, she continued:

"You didn't have friends in then. Party got a bit rowdy, perhaps? Is it just the two of you here?"

Sarah intervened. "No, we didn't have friends in, at all. And yes, it is just the two of us here. He's my brother."

"I see." Then, after another pause, "It's a one-bedroomed flat, isn't it? Where do you sleep, Sarah?"

Tom leapt in. "Why on earth are you asking that? I thought you were here because of a complaint about noise. Now you are asking about our sleeping arrangements. I don't know what you think you're getting at but since you ask, Sarah sleeps on the sofa. Is there anything else?" he asked dismissively.

Joanne was not so easily dismissed. "How old are you Sarah?"

"Fifteen," was the brief reply.

"Where do you go to school," now asked Joanne.

Another brief reply: "Jevington."

After some hesitation, Joanne commented, "That's a long way to travel. Do they take day pupils?"

Tom leapt in again. One thing St. Illtyd's had succeeded in imbuing in Tom was a manner of self-assurance accompanied by the appropriate voice typical of public schools:

"I really don't know what this is all about; why you're asking all these questions. But if you must know, Sarah was pissed off with Jevington and left. We had a God almighty row with our mother about it and we, my sister and I, decided that the best solution was for Sarah to come and live with me until we got things sorted out. She will be registering with a local school as soon as we can arrange it. Is this a police matter? What are you really here for?"

Police-sergeant Helby found herself asking the same question:

"I'm sorry to have bothered you. As I say, we had a complaint about excessive noise but it must clearly have come from another flat." She rose to go. At the door, she turned and said, "Sarah had better be sure to register at her new school as soon as possible or your next visit might be from the Attendance Officer."

She knew how unlikely this was. Kids regularly left school at fifteen, if a job was offered for example, and nobody did anything about it. But the warning enabled her to leave with her authority intact.

After she had left, Tom and Sarah looked at one another. It was clear to them that the proffered excuse for the visit was a load of nonsense. The line of questioning left them in no doubt what the true purpose of the visit had been. They were not greatly concerned. They were satisfied that their explanation had convinced the police, at least for the time being. But they wondered who their accuser had been and realised that they had not necessarily yet seen the end of it all. It seemed likely that as long as they were living in the flat in Warwick there was always the danger of another visit, this time, perhaps, by better-informed investigators.

The following morning, Police-sergeant Joanne Helby rang Alice Walker at Social Services:

"Well, I called at the Foresters' flat yesterday evening and, to be honest, I didn't get anywhere. They have a perfectly plausible explanation for their situation –Sarah pissed off with Jevington, stomps out, row at home, walks out etc. All the same, I'm not wholly convinced. It's the shagging that bothers me. Are we sure about it? I suggest you have another chat with the neighbour, this Angela girl. See if she's convincing. If she is, we need to carry the investigation further. See what we can find out. This time we'll need to be a bit more subtle about it."

Alice concurred. That was the course they decided upon.

By the time they next spoke to Angela, the

Forester flat was already vacant. Tom and Sarah had packed their bags that evening after the police visit. They filled the car and headed off first thing the following morning stopping off at the house only long enough to collect passports. Vittoria tried to ask them where they were going and what was happening. They did not tell her.

They headed to Folkestone, got a train almost immediately and that evening arrived at the *manoir* near Pont-Farcy. It was to become their home for some time. There was a difference, however, between occupying the *manoir* for a few carefree weeks in the sun each summer and living there as fugitives from justice.

Their discontent with their situation became greatly aggravated when Sarah concluded that she was pregnant. She had wondered for a few weeks before they fled; now it seemed clearly the case. It posed the question of where and how to have the baby when the time came.

Police surveillance of the Warwick flat eventually led to the conclusion that there was nothing to survey. The occupants had departed. No-one knew where they had gone. No-one knew if and when they would be back. The police however drew the inference that they had something to flee from. There must have been some sort of sex-related illegal activity after all.

CHAPTER TEN

Sarah and Tom ruled out the idea of having the baby in France. They were just too ignorant about the system. For a time, they considered the extreme solution of moving to Dubai. Tom actually wrote to his father, a rare event, to ask how he would feel about him and Sarah moving there. He did not mention the relationship, which he enjoyed with Sarah, let alone her pregnancy. That would have complicated things unduly and could be dealt with later if necessary.

Andrew's reply was as expected. He discussed it with Sally. "Discussed" is perhaps not quite the right word since there really was nothing to discuss. In particular, there was no way they were ever going to assume responsibility for Tom, let alone an abducted child. Both thought it a thoroughly bad idea and Andrew tactfully let Tom know that that was the case.

Sarah and Tom eventually concluded that their best course was to return to the United Kingdom for Sarah to have the baby. They could wait a few more weeks and it would not be a good idea to return to Warwick where they might again attract the interest of the Social Services Department. They briefly considered the idea of asylum with their 'grandmother', Rosalie, but she had been consistent in making it clear that she wanted nothing to do with

Sarah. What the reason was, neither of them had ever understood though the reasons were about to become clear.

Although it was not an attractive prospect, the best idea of a bad lot seemed to be to for them to make peace with their mother and throw themselves on her mercy. However disgruntled Kate was with the whole business, there was absolutely nothing she could do about it. The very last thing their mother was going to do was to involve the police and/or the social services.

Kate was at work when they returned. Vittoria was astonished to see them when she threw open the door. Her emotions were mixed. She loved them both; they were like her own children and indeed they had spent more of their lives in the company of Vittoria and Bella than they had with their "mother". At the same time, Vittoria foresaw trouble when Kate returned home and when Tom and Sarah explained the situation she became distressed. She scented the whiff of disaster in the air and felt utterly helpless in the face of it.

And well she might. As Kate drove into the drive she saw a Renault Clio parked there. She immediately recognised it as Tom's and girded up her loins for the inevitable confrontation, which was about to happen. She let herself in, dropped off her bag and coat and headed to the kitchen. There they all were, Tom, Sarah, Vittoria and Bella, all looking

103

extremely apprehensive. Kate was not amused, was not pleased to see them. Without any greeting she launched straight in:

"Well! Come to your senses have you?"

At first no-one spoke. Bella temporised with "A cup of tea, anyone?" and was ignored. Kate, as yet unaware of Sarah's pregnancy, spoke again:

"God knows what a mess you've got yourselves into. You know we've had social services, AND the police here. They got the address from Jevington. I have never been more embarrassed in my life."

Still no-one else spoke. Each seemed to be waiting for someone else to reply. Kate carried on:

"Right! Well it's clear we've got to do what we can retrieve the situation. Sarah - you're going back to Jevington, if I can persuade them to take you back. They probably will; they'll think of the money. And you Tom, you're off back to Warwick – if they'll take you back, which I very much doubt. It will help if Dr. Smythe can bring himself to diagnose a nervous breakdown..."

Tom interrupted her: "Sarah's pregnant."

At first, Kate was speechless and they all waited for the reaction. It came:

"What?! She can't be."

"She is," calmly affirmed Vittoria.

"Well she'll have to get rid of it," announced Kate, as though Sarah were not there.

"She can't," continued Vittoria, quietly, "She's too far gone."

"When is it due?" Kate finally acknowledged Sarah's interest.

"About six or seven weeks, as far as I can tell," Sarah informed her.

"Christ, what a mess!" said Kate. "Have any of you thought what you're going to do?" as though it were as much Vittoria's and Bella's concern as well as Tom and Sarah's. Kate herself had no idea. She continued:

"I fucking warned you about this, didn't I? And you took no fucking notice. Well, you got yourselves into this mess; you get yourselves out of it!" and with that, she stomped out of the room. She knew, however, that it was a mess in which she too might become dangerously involved.

The remaining four looked at one another. Vittoria and Bella could not offer any useful advice. They did not feel free to do so. Tom and Sarah stared at one another, but only briefly. Then Tom nodded towards the door and said to Sarah, "Come on. This is no place for us."

Vittoria said, "No, you must stay here. Where will you go?"

"Back to the flat in Warwick," said Tom.

"But what about the police; that social worker?"

"We'll take that as it comes," replied Tom.

Sarah nodded assent. "Things will have quietened down by now. And in any case, Sarah will be sixteen in a few days; she'll be free to do whatever she wants. We shall get married as soon as we can. The money's no problem, thanks to Forester's."

Vittoria said in a hushed voice, "but she'll still be your sister, won't she. You won't be able to get married; they won't allow it. And in any case, the Register office would not marry Sarah, even at sixteen. She would have to have her parents' consent."

"Who gives a fuck about that?" threw in Tom. "Nobody will bother us."

He was to be proved to be wrong about that.

Sarah and Tom picked up their bags and headed for the front door. Kate interrupted them: "Where do you think you're going?" she almost yelled at them.

"As if you give a damn about anyone but yourself," was Tom's reply as they left the house and climbed into the Clio.

Kate did, of course, care about herself, but only she knew why.

CHAPTER ELEVEN

Tom and Sarah duly returned to Warwick and settled into the flat again. One of the first to notice was their neighbour, Angela, although it was to be some weeks before anyone else took a renewed interest.

They registered immediately with a local medical practice, "The Eaves" where it was confirmed that Sarah was due to give birth in a matter of five or so weeks. Arrangements were made for the baby to be delivered in a private maternity hospital nearby. The Forester fortune could afford it.

When the time came the baby was duly delivered, pretty much as predicted. Sarah had a rough time of it but survived well enough without being greatly excited about now having a baby daughter. It was not something she had wanted and she wished she had taken greater care to avoid it. Nor was it something for which Tom had mentally prepared himself. It had not been in their plans and they were still mystified as to how it had happened.

When Sarah returned to the flat with the baby, it gradually dawned on them both that their lives had changed irreversibly and that life at the flat would never again be as easy and relaxed as it had been during their first residency there. The contrast was particularly marked at night. It was no longer a matter of having a loving fuck and falling asleep in each other's arms.

For a not uncommon congeries of reasons, Sarah did not now want to have sex. She had been hurt by the birth and was only slowly recovering. The baby was not accommodating. It took several feeds each night to stifle its cries even for short periods and Sarah was exhausted by it all. And Tom was not much help. He girded up his loins and learned to change nappies but otherwise was of little use. He had not bargained for any of this. Most of the time, he was not even there. There was nothing to be gained by his choosing to mooch about the flat. That was now hardly an entertaining activity.

With Dr. Smythe's help he had got his place back at university and attending lectures and tutorials plus working in the library meant that Sarah was left alone with her charge for the greater part of the day. She knew no-one in the town. She resented Tom's absences and the burden of caring for the child, which was consequently thrust unfairly on her. For the first time in their relationship a wedge had been driven between them and it was firmly fixed in. It eventually ended in their separation.

Hitherto, apart from the late intervention of the police and social worker, the relationship between Tom and Sarah had been largely pure, innocent and uncomplicated and had come to depend largely on sex. Parenthood had seriously infected this settled state of affairs. A further infection was to have a lethal effect.

Angela had twice bumped into Tom on the way to university. On the first occasion, she had started out by being distant and uncommunicative and had been surprised to note that Tom was more forthcoming than had ever previously been the case. On his part, Tom had never forgotten the occasion when Angela had appeared to offer herself to him and now found himself regretting that he had been so dismissive of her approach.

She was an attractive girl and Tom was surprised to find himself imagining having sex with her. He had never previously taken a serious interest in any other woman. Sarah had been more than enough for him but now she was no longer, at least for the time being, available and Tom was unaccustomed to celibacy especially when, as was increasingly the case, it was accompanied by rancour.

On the second occasion on which Tom and Angela met, they interrupted their walk into the university to have a coffee and a chat in a local café. The topic of the newly-arrived child arose and the conversation led imperceptibly to Tom's frustration.

"It's normal, I suppose, but I can see that it would be difficult," commented Angela.

"I have to say, I don't rate being a father much. It was never something we had in mind. Just something one has to put up with, I suppose," replied Tom, adding, "Though it's not easy."

"I can see that," continued Angela. "Look, I

have to dash or I shall be late, but if you'd like to talk more about it, why don't you pop in. I'm only next door after all; we could have a drink and a chat."

Given their history, albeit brief, the message was not lost on Tom.

Predictably it turned out to be more than a drink and a chat. Sarah had taken the baby to the maternity clinic and would be gone for at least a couple of hours. Tom went straight next door and knocked. Angela expressed a delighted surprise to see him and ushered him in. Had she known he was coming, she thought, she would have dressed more invitingly, but she did the best she could in the circumstances and excused herself:

"Sorry, I've just been clearing up some of the mess. Can I get you a beer while I tidy myself up and slip into something more comfortable?"

She fetched Tom a cool beer from the Kitchen and then headed for her bedroom She did not bother to close the bedroom door. More accurately, she deliberately left it open and made sure that Tom could see her as she shed her blouse and jeans. Seeing her there wearing nothing but her underwear wholly reduced the attractions of a beer and without comment he stood and headed for the bedroom. Angela stood expectantly by the bed and immediately responded when Tom put his arms around her and kissed her. They fell on the bed and Angela experienced a moment of triumph as Tom unclipped her bra and pulled off her knickers. She unfastened his belt and pushed his jeans and pants down but only as far as his thighs. It was enough. A long-awaited revenge fuck was on its way.

The inevitable happened.

Tom had hardly come before he began to experience feelings of remorse. He silently pulled up his pants and jeans and, fastening his belt as he went, left Angela's flat almost immediately without a word. She, having initially felt triumphant, suddenly felt doubly-scorned. She took a shower, dressed and without a moment's hesitation phoned Alice Walker at the Social Services Department. She reintroduced herself:

"I don't know if you remember me but I spoke to you some months ago about the situation in the flat next door to mine…"

"Angela, yes, I remember," Alice interrupted her. "Yes, we looked into it. You were right to draw it to our attention and we decided it was something we ought to follow up but when we went back to the flat they had gone. We tried several times but they were never there."

"Yes," continued Angela, "they were away for a long while but they're back and… well… there seems to be a baby. I don't know anything more than that, whether it's theirs or not but… well I thought you should know."

"Yes, indeed. Thank you Angela. Obviously

we'd better have another look at it."

And they did. Alice and Joanne Helby called at the flat the following morning. Tom had left; Sarah was there alone with the baby. Yes, it was her's and Tom's. They would be getting married as soon as they could...

"But you can't get married, can you" Joanne pointed out. "You're brother and sister aren't you? A brother and sister can't marry, you must know that. It's within what the law calls 'the prohibited degrees of consanguinity'".

"I don't care what the law calls it. Tom and I love each other," (though she surprised herself by experiencing, for the first time, a smidgeon of doubt about that as she said it) "and that's that."

"I'm afraid it isn't," Alice contradicted her. "You absolutely cannot go on like this. Do you realise that you're committing a very serious crime – incest. You cannot stay here with Tom. It has to stop, immediately."

"If you continue to live with Tom," added Joanne, "that will be something we cannot ignore. Do you understand what I'm saying? You must sort it out with Tom when he gets back. The obvious thing is for you to go with the baby and live with your mother. You cannot go on living with Tom. I can see that will be hard for you, but you really have no choice. You absolutely must tell Tom when he gets back. I have to warn you that if you persist in living as you do we shall have no recourse other than to pursue the matter."

She did not specify what 'pursuing the matter' might consist of but Sarah understood, as did Tom when she recounted the day's events on his return, that whatever it consisted of, it meant a break-up of their relationship and Sarah was not yet prepared to contemplate that.

Police-sergeant Joanne Helby did her best to ensure the right outcome. She arranged to see Kate that evening and laid it all out:

"We made it as clear to them as we possibly could but they seem determined to stay together. I have to tell you that if they do, we shall have no choice but to prosecute – certainly Tom; we're not sure about Sarah."

"Christ!" said Kate. Joanne reasonably assumed that Kate's concern was for her children. She did not appreciate that Kate had concerns of her own. Kate and a very few others knew that Tom and Sarah were not brother and sister but the possible consequences of such a revelation were terrifying.

"I'll go and see them. See if I can knock some sense into them. I'll go tomorrow, first thing; can you hold off until then?"

"Of course. I hope you can get them to see straight," said Joanne, and with that she left to return to Warwick.

Kate arrived at the flat at 8:30 a.m. the

113

following morning. She knocked on the door. It did not open. Instead she heard Tom's voice, apprehensive lest the police and social worker were outside:

"Who's there?"

"It's me, your mother. Please let me in; I must talk to you."

Tom opened the door. "What do you want?"

"Please let me in. You must listen to me... "

Kate heard Sarah's voice:

"Who is it?"

Tom answered by allowing Kate to enter.

"Listen to me. The police have been to see me. They made it clear in no uncertain terms that if you carry on like this, they will prosecute you for incest. Do you understand what that means? Prison and a criminal record. And think of the publicity. Think of the harm it will do to my practice..."

Tom groaned as he interrupted: "Here we go again; always thinking of how things will affect you. What about us?"

Kate continued: "It's you I'm thinking about. At least let's try and stave off the immediate crisis. We don't have to decide anything final, now. For the moment, just think of the short term. Tom – you should go and stay with your grandmother at The Poplars if you want to get away from here. Sarah, you and the baby can come home with me, now. Vittoria will be a great help with the baby..."

"And then what?" chipped in Sarah. "Your so-called 'short-term' solution looks very like your long-term plan to me."

"We're not going anywhere," said Tom. "The police don't prosecute incest anymore… "

"They say they will," insisted Kate.

"Well we'll cross that bridge when we come to it," asserted Tom.

"Don't you realise? You're at the bridge now. The police will be here later today. Unless we sort it, NOW, you'll be arrested. You'll be prosecuted. You'll have no defence." (At least, not one you are going to be enabled to mount, thought Kate to herself).

Tom went to the door, opened it and said "Go home; or to your precious office or wherever. Sarah and I are staying here – together. We don't need you; we can look after ourselves."

Kate had tried wheedling and persuading. Now she lost it. As she headed for the door, she turned: "You're so fucking stubborn; so fucking stupid. I've done my best. You deserve everything you get. I wash my hands of you," and with that she slammed the door and left.

CHAPTER TWELVE

Back at her office, Kate phoned Joanne Helby:

"Well, I went to the flat first thing this morning and tried to knock some sense into them."

"And?" queried Joanne.

"Well I think I knocked — I hope I knocked some sense into them."

"So Sarah's coming to you and Tom to his grandmother's, is that what's happening?"

Kate paused, uncertain. Then: "Not yet; but I'm sure they're thinking about it."

"So they haven't agreed to sort it out," said Joanne.

"Not yet. But given a bit of time to mull it over I think they'll see sense."

"I'm sorry Mrs. Forester, but sense has been staring them in the face for ages and from what you're saying they haven't seen it yet."

"Oh, I'm sure they will, given time... "

"As I say, Mrs. Forester, I'm sorry but time has run out. We can't go on ignoring it. The whole time they spend together in that flat — now with a child! — They are continuing to commit a very serious crime. We shall be arresting them today."

"Please... "

"Good-bye, Mrs. Forester," said Joanne and put the phone down.

Tom did not go to university that day. Mid-

116

afternoon, two police cars pulled up outside. There was a knock on the door of the flat. Tom asked:

"Who is it?"

Joanne replied, "Police. Open the door, please."

Until that moment, Tom and Sarah had not really believed it would happen. Tom opened the door and Joanne Helby, Alice Walker and two police constables entered. Joanne did not hold back:

"Thomas Forester, Sarah Forester, I'm arresting you for the crime of incest. Thomas Forester, I am also arresting you for having unlawful carnage knowledge of a minor." She proceeded to caution them. The police constables led away Tom. Alice addressed Sarah:

"Can you get the baby's things together please, Sarah?" Sarah did so; and off they all went.

There had been some discussion with the Crown Prosecution Service about charges. Incest prosecutions were rare. Such issues were usually resolved without needing to proceed as far as trial. Here, however, Joanne pointed out, they had tried every means to put an end to the illegal affair and had failed. Prosecution might well be a last resort in such cases, but that was where they were now.

There was further debate about the unlawful knowledge charge. Nobody prosecuted eighteen year olds for having sex with fifteen year olds nowadays. If they did, the prisons would be full.

"This is different," pointed out Joanne. "I know there aren't many fifteen year old virgins around these days but not many of them lost it shagging their older brothers. We 'd like both charges – we'd like to be sure that the arrogant bastard gets it one way or another."

The Crown Prosecution Service agreed to proceed on both counts. There was abundant evidence, or so they thought, and it was definitely not in the public interest to allow incest to proceed unchecked in any way.

Alice contacted Kate who willingly undertook to take charge of Sarah and the baby so bail was granted for her. Tom, however, was refused bail. The two of them had already skipped the jurisdiction in order to avoid prosecution on a previous occasion and Tom was detained in custody.

The Forester fortune could afford the best lawyers. Their own solicitors already qualified under this heading and they recommended Julian Edwards Q.C. who took on the defence.

At the first conference he listened patiently to Tom's and then Sarah's account of events. The outcome of this was positive for Sarah. Edwards contacted the Crown Prosecution Service informally and put it to them that Sarah, three years younger than Tom, had been a passive, ignorant and innocent victim in the affair. Charges against her were dropped.

Tom's case was altogether more problematic. A second conference led to Edwards' advice that Tom's best course was to plead guilty. Edwards would argue his youth and ignorance in mitigation and hope for a light sentence. It was at this point that Kate shook them all by asking:

"Would it make any difference if they had different fathers?"

"What do you mean?" asked a puzzled Edwards.

"Tom's father is not Sarah's father," said Kate.

"Well, it would still be incest," said Edwards, "but it could be useful in mitigation. Are you willing to tell us who her father is?"

"I don't have much choice, do I?" commented Kate "but actually there's not a lot I can tell you. Sarah is the product of a one-night stand I had nearly seventeen years ago. I flew back from Dubai with him, we got talking on the plane and the rest followed – in an airport hotel after we landed."

"Are you still in touch?" asked Edwards.

"No, I haven't seen him since. All I know is that his first name was Alex. I never knew his second name. He was an Edinburgh advocate – that's all I ever knew about him. It's not something I'm proud of; it was a very stressful time, divorce etc. I persuaded my former husband to acknowledge the child, but she's not his."

Kate had not really thought about it. It was a

spur of the moment thing, almost an aside born out of desperation. She regretted it immediately when the talk turned to identification and DNA tests.

She became evasive. She had had no contact with the father since. She did not know his address. She could remember no details of the date or flight. They would just have to take her word for it... But they could not. She was forced to give them an approximate date. They had her full name and this enabled Emirates to track down the flight manifest. There were not all that many in business class and only one "Alexander", Alexander Forsyth who, it turned out, was a member of the Edinburgh bar.

It was easy to track him down although he was far from pleased to have an illicit shag from seventeen years ago dragged up. Eventually, granted an undertaking of confidence – it did not matter, no-one would ever know – he agreed to give a DNA sample. Without really understanding what it was about, Sarah also agreed to a sample.

The samples proved conclusively that Forsyth was not Sarah's father. That avenue was closed but the issues, which it raised, were not resolved.

"Forgive me for asking," said Edwards, "but who is the father of your child, Sarah?"

Kate now wished she had never gone down that road. She put an end to it by blithely stating "Oh, I always thought it was Alex... this is something I really don't want to go into ... but there were a number of one night stands at the time. It was a difficult time for me. I was a bit off the rails for a time..."

"Can you tell us who they were?" persisted Edwards. "Names, addresses, whatever."

"I'm afraid I can't. It was an awful time. They were just men I picked up in restaurants, clubs, et cetera..." Edwards was old enough and wise enough to doubt whilst keeping his doubts to himself. It was a wholly unsatisfactory state of affairs. That, however, looked like the end of that particular road.

Then the solicitors unexpectedly received an anonymous letter.

It was unsigned, but its anonymity was, for Kate, somewhat compromised by the fact that it emanated from Dubai. There were only two possible sources and she knew perfectly well which one was responsible for it.

It stated simply:

"Sarah is not Tom's sister."

When first tackled with this, Kate's response was that it was nonsense. They should not be taking any notice of an anonymous letter. When asked if she had any idea who might have sent it, Kate was forced to admit that her ex-husband was domiciled in Dubai and it might well have come from him, though why he would say this and, especially, if he had something to say, why he would do so anonymously, she could not say.

Kate did not tell them what she knew. It was that "Paki-bitch", wasn't it? Andrew must have told her. She didn't give a fuck about Tom. She was just sticking the knife in now she had the chance.

Kate thought long and hard. All was not done yet. She had cleverly anticipated this situation seventeen years earlier. She inwardly congratulated herself on her foresight.

"Alright," she told them in the conference. "I was hoping to God this would never come out. It really puts the cat among the pigeons but we seem to have no choice now. Sarah is not my child."

A stunned silence followed. Then Edwards spoke:

"Are you telling us that Tom and Sarah are not brother and sister?"

"Yes, I am."

There were audible gasps all round the table. Edwards continued:

"You were willing to let your son... I presume Tom is your son, is he?... You were willing to let your son go to prison when you knew all along that there was no incest involved?"

"No. Definitely not. I would have revealed everything if and when it came to the crunch. I was hoping it would not."

Another silence followed. Then Edwards took it up again.

"I take it we shall be able to prove all this. DNA

tests should establish once and for all that they are not siblings. But who is Sarah if she's not your daughter? That's the question everybody will be asking and we'd better have an answer."

Kate had her answer all ready. It had been ready for just this contingency all those years:

"Sarah is a foundling."

More expressions of astonishment followed this claim.

"She was on the porch-step, in a bassinet, when I came home from work. I can give you the precise date."

It was a precise date, but only because Kate had selected it as being precisely two days after the Powell Street abduction.

"I still have the bassinet. It's in the garage at home. And I have kept the note."

"What note?" asked Edwards.

"The note left with the baby – in the bassinet. I'll get it and show it to you."

There was indeed a note. It was sixteen years old. It was written in capital letters in a crude hand with a ball-point pen on a leaf apparently torn out of a school notebook. The 'crude hand' was in fact Kate's left hand. It read, simply:

"PLEASE LOOK AFTER MY BABY. I CANT. I KNOW YOUR RICH. I KNOW YOU CAN AFFORD IT. IF YOU WONT I SHALL KILL MYSELF."

Kate was quite proud of this effort. Whilst not

ambidextrous, her facility with her other hand was sufficient to put doubters off the trail. And the misspellings were subtle and not so glaring as to raise doubts.

Back in conference again, Kate showed them the note. Mindful of the notion that admitting to a minor vice renders one's denial of a major one more credible, she confessed that she had always wanted a daughter – people would tell them that she was always going on about it. Possibly that might have influenced her decision but that was not the main reason for it, she asserted.

"What would you have done?" she asked. "Would you have risked the poor girl killing herself? I thought about it long and hard, I can tell you. But she was right. I am rich. I could give the child a home and a good upbringing. I knew there would be problems but I thought I could solve them all. I thought I had done."

Edwards was clearly sceptical but Sarah's origins were not the crucial point:

"Well, I have no idea what people will make of this but it need not concern us, at least so far as Tom's trial is concerned. When they get the DNA tests, the Crown Prosecution Service will drop the incest charge. They'll have no choice. Tom will still have to answer the unlawful carnal knowledge charge. He has no defence; he'll have to plead guilty but I think there's a very good chance of his getting at worst a suspended sentence. He'll have a criminal record, of course, and he'll be on the register of offenders for a good spell but that's the best we can hope for."

Edwards' predictions turned out to be correct. The incest charge was dropped; Tom pleaded guilty to the unlawful carnal knowledge charge and was duly convicted with the consequences accurately forecast by Edwards. There were, however, other consequences.

CHAPTER THIRTEEN

George Forester's role as major supplier of cocaine had gained him entrée into what passed for high society in Birmingham. Of course, the Forester money helped, as did the Bentley Continental. Moving in those circles, he met Val. She was a loving and sensible girl and brought some stability to George's life for a number of years during most of which he managed to stay out of prison. He did not need to deal in drugs for the money. His father's legacy had left him comfortably off and there would be more to come when his mother died. But being a chief supplier of cocaine to what passed for the haut monde of Birmingham, accompanied by his obvious wealth gave him a status that he greatly appreciated.

It could not go on forever and inevitably the police eventually identified him as a major dealer. Another term of imprisonment, this time four years, followed. When he was released, two and a half years later, Val, who had visited him regularly, was waiting for him at the prison gates. She was not alone in drawing a distinction between activities in which many thousands engaged for innocent pleasure on the one hand and rape and bloody murder on the other, when it came to what was to be treated as being criminal. For her, George was not a criminal. He was a "fun guy", victimised by the authorities and she loved him.

126

What she did not love was the long separation brought about by his spell in prison. Now that he was again a free man she wanted him to remain so. It was not as if he needed to deal in drugs for the money. She knew that he was very comfortably off with his inheritance, which had been greatly bolstered when he had reached twenty-three and received the capital under his father's trust. Dealing had become a habit – a way of accommodating his friends. He had no need for financial gain.

Val, bringing the love of a good woman to bear, had no difficulty persuading George that it would be a good idea to abandon dealing in drugs but he viewed with dismay the prospect of doing nothing. Yes, he should try to establish a new career. But what? He had no qualifications, hardly any skills. Starting at the bottom of anything was singularly lacking in appeal.

They sat there after dinner at the Metropole quaffing the last of a bottle of Vosne Romanee contemplating the problem. Suddenly, Val said:

"Wine."

"Wine what?" queried George.

"We could produce wine," explained Val. "Buy a vineyard somewhere."

"We haven't a clue about wine except how to drink it," commented George.

"That doesn't matter. We can buy expertise while we're learning the business. You're not short of money, after all."

Imperceptibly the idea took root. "Where?" asked George.

"That's something we'd have to think about, but what about it?"

The idea grew. They thought about it. They ended up as owners of a medium-sized vineyard near Angers in the Coteaux d'Ancenis. It was barely profitable. Its owner was seeking to retire but was more than willing to stay on as a paid consultant for as long as George and Val required. The other staff, who had been apprehensive about unemployment, were relieved to continue in work. To their way of thinking, total abandonment of the vineyard had been a distinct possibility.

As befitted their status as owners, George and Val moved into the small chateau. The former owner and his wife occupied the large home-farmhouse, which had recently become vacant.

It seemed like, indeed it was, the ideal arrangement. The vineyard offered a little-known *appellation* but that was positive. It meant not only that they got a lot for their money but also that it gave them something to strive for. They grew mainly *sauvignon blanc* and *gamay*. George's last, brief, flirtation with criminality was to speculate to Val about relabeling their product. There was already, said George, more "Sancerre" in the world than could possibly be produced there. Clearly a lot of people were at it; why not them? And Beaujolais Villages such as *Morgon* and *Chiroubles* were becoming increasingly popular. Some surreptitious relabeling would increase their profits substantially.

Val immediately scotched the idea:

"The French take that sort of fraud extremely seriously. We could both end up in some unsavoury French prison for years and years."

Besides, that was, in her mind, "proper" crime, unlike supplying cocaine which did little harm and gave pleasure to her friends and lots of other people.

Over the years, George came to lead a "normal" life. He and Val married and had two children. He became absorbed in his business. They steadily improved the quality of the wine, mainly by more careful harvesting and the business became slightly more profitable although they were never going to make millions. They did not need to. They already had millions. They were well enough off to be able to take frequent breaks and explore the gastronomy of the Loire and Brittany. They even persuaded a Michelin-starred restaurant near Rennes to feature their products on its wine-list. This gave George more of a kick than any drug ever had.

George had, though, continued to be estranged from his mother, Rosalie, and his sister Kate. On his release after serving a third term in prison he had returned to The Poplars only for his mother to refuse him admission and tell him she never wanted to see him again. Kate's reaction had been similar. Now, several years into his career as an honest *vigneron*, George decided to make an attempt at reconciliation. He actually felt proud of what he and Val had achieved and hoped for something resembling recognition from his mother and sister. And besides, they had never met Val, whom he was sure his mother would take to, or, more particularly, the two new Forester grandchildren.

He sent both his mother and Kate a case of *gamay* and a case of *sauvignon blanc* accompanied by only a short note explaining, in a few brief sentences, his career over the years since they had last been in contact and wishing them enjoyment of the product of which he and his wife Val were proud.

Rosalie was touched. George's early criminal career had eventually left her almost completely socially isolated and the presence of Sarah in Kate's household had meant that, apart from occasional "duty" visits by Kate and Tom, she rarely saw any of them. George's early career had never ceased to hurt but now it actually appeared that he had successfully "gone straight" and was back "on track". She replied thanking them and expressing the hope that they might visit The Poplars so that she could meet Val and the two grandchildren of whose existence she had theretofore been unaware.

Kate never acknowledged receipt of the wine though she drank it.

As the weeks went by without any acknowledgement from Kate, George came more and more to seethe with resentment. Yes, he had done time in prison but her criminality, if such it was (and he had become increasingly sure of the fact as the years rolled by with no solution to the mystery of the Powell Street abduction) was in an altogether different league. He reckoned he knew what she had done. Had known for sixteen years. On his third release from prison, Rosalie had turned him away and he had headed for Kate's hoping for temporary refuge there until he found his feet again.

She had not been in but he had waited in the Merc. just up the street. He had seen her arrive home and he got out of his car to head for the house. Turning into the drive, he stopped, curious at what was going on. Kate had unloaded the boot placing various objects on the porch and had then opened the passenger door and lifted out – a baby! Kate did not have a baby. She had, he knew, a son, Tom, about three years old by now but she had divorced his father over a year ago.

George made a possible connection immediately. Kate had always wanted a daughter. He had heard, on the car radio, just minutes before, the news of the abduction of a baby in Powell Street. It had been the main headline on the news. He waited until Kate closed the front door behind her, then went back to the Merc. and drove off. He had a lengthy criminal record. The last thing he wanted to do was to risk being connected to a serious crime of an altogether different dimension.

Although he had made the connection, George could not credit that Kate was the perpetrator of the abduction and remained unsure until very many years afterwards. It was only when he and his family eventually found time to visit Rosalie that the last bricks were put in place. Sitting round the log fire with brandies after dinner, George asked his mother about his sister:

"I tried to make contact with her, you know. Sent a couple of cases of wine to her when I sent them to you, but I never heard a thing from her."

"No, you wouldn't," said Rosemary. "I hardly ever see her. I don't know what I've done wrong," she added, knowing of course that it was Kate who had done wrong but hesitant about broaching the subject with George.

A short silence ensued, each wondering whether to take the conversation further. Eventually George spoke:

"There's something that's always puzzled me about Kate. A weird thing happened... you remember... I came out of jail for the third time and you turned me away..."

Rosemary started an explanation "I..." but got no further. George continued:

"No, it's alright. It doesn't matter. Water under

the bridge, now, but after I left you, I headed off for Kate's. Hoped she would be a bit more forgiving... sorry! I didn't mean..."

"That's OK. Fair enough," interjected Rosalie.

"Anyway, it was at the time of that abduction in Powell Street. I don't know if you remember it..."

Rosalie knew what was coming. "I remember it very well."

"Well, I was just heading towards the house. Kate was unloading her car – she unloaded a baby! Can you imagine? I'd just heard about the Powell Street business on the car radio and I knew nothing about Kate having a baby; we were all, you remember, out of touch at that time but I couldn't help but wonder... "

"She took it." There was a long pause.

"Seriously, she did?"

"Yes."

"She told you?"

"Yes." Rosalie hesitated before continuing, "she put me in an impossible position. There was Alex to worry about. You weren't exactly covering yourself with glory at the time. If I hadn't kept my mouth shut, Kate would have gone to prison as well and her career would have been ruined. And there was Tom to think of – what would have happened to him?"

"So she's got away with it?"

"Just," said Rosalie.

"What does 'just' mean?" asked George and

Rosalie proceeded to explain at length the events surrounding Tom and Sarah's affair.

"Christ Almighty," was George's comment. "And they believed her, about the baby being a foundling, I mean?"

"Apparently. No-one ever linked it to the abduction."

"So she got away with it?"

"Yes."

"So far," muttered George under his breath.

CHAPTER FOURTEEN

Joining Val in bed, George recounted the conversation he had had with his mother.

"Good God!" exclaimed Val. "I remember it well. I was still at school. Oh, the poor parents! It's... it's as good as murder. What an awful thing to have done... and she's got away with it!"

Kate's rejection of her brother had not endeared her to Val. Quite the opposite. "And you've being doing time for peanuts while she's got away with murder!"

"Do you think we should do something about it?" asked George.

Val did not hesitate. "Yes, absolutely. Fuck Kate! Those parents are entitled to have their child back, even if it has been sixteen years or so. If you don't tell the police, I will."

On the morning when they left to return to France, George went to the car to use the French carphone. He rang the Birmingham police. He had his statement ready. Ignoring requests for name and address he spoke quickly but clearly:

"The baby abducted from Powell Street sixteen years ago is still alive as Sarah Jane Forester, daughter of Katherine Forester, the architect," and switched off the phone.

Sarah Jane Ferguson was soon identified by the Birmingham police as the girl who had been

135

involved in an incest inquiry in Warwick and they contacted the Warwick police. It soon reached Joanne Helby's desk. She immediately contacted Alice Walker and filled her in. Alice replied:

"I never did believe that bollocks about the foundling business, did you?"

"It seemed a very unlikely story."

"So what do we do?"

The first and most obvious thing to do was to check it out. It was an anonymous phone call. They thought it might have come from overseas but they had not been able to trace it. Still, the course was simple. They needed to take DNA samples of Sarah and the parents of the abducted child.

Sarah was still trying to become adjusted to the fact that she was a foundling – did not know who her parents were. She was highly suspicious when Joanne and Alice contacted her yet again but she said nothing to Kate. They were far from being on the best of terms. Joanne and Alice arranged to collect her while Kate was at work. They fobbed off her questions in the car and drove her to the Social Care Department in Warwick. There, they had a delicate task to perform but the best course seemed to be to come straight to the point. Alice told her:

"We may have found your true parents."

Sarah was taken aback. "You know who they are?"

"We're not absolutely sure. We have to check,

136

but we think we do. We need you to take a DNA test to see if there is a match."

Perhaps surprisingly Sarah was hesitant at first. But she was not sure she wanted to know. She was still adjusting to losing one set of 'parents' and here she was, being offered a new set. But, after a pause, she agreed.

It took a little time for the Birmingham police to track down Karen and Sean Ferguson. They were no longer at their old address. Sean was easily found at Ferguson Tyres and Exhausts and he was able to direct them to Karen's mother's address. They dealt with Sean first.

"So what's this about?" he asked.

They did their best to prepare him for the shock then Alice told him straight out:

"We think we may have found your daughter."

Sean was initially puzzled. "Found my daughter. I didn't know she was lost."

"Your daughter Sonya who was abducted… sixteen years ago."

It took some time to sink in. "Christ! I thought she was dead."

"Well, it has been a long time."

"Good Lord. After all this time. Are you sure?"

"Well, we're not absolutely certain. That's why we're here. We want you to take a DNA test. That should settle it one way or another."

That was no problem.

Dealing with Karen was different. They knocked at the door of the run-down terrace house. Karen opened the door to find herself confronting two women, one a policewoman. She immediately jumped to the wrong conclusion:

"She's dead, isn't she? You've found her at last." Karen broke down in tears.

"No, we don't believe she's dead. We think she's alive. May we come in?"

Karen was momentarily frozen with incomprehension and incredulity. Then she came round and ushered them in, impatiently expectant. The interior of the house was as depressing as its exterior. Karen sat them down and waited anxiously. Alice told her:

"We think Sonya may be alive; we think we've found her."

Karen did not even hear the second part of the sentence. "She's alive!" she exclaimed. "I knew it. I've always known it..."

Alice interrupted: "I said we THINK we've found her. We have to make sure."

Karen leapt at the suggestion of a DNA test. She wanted to know more. "When can I see her?"

"As soon as we've made certain that it is Sonya, we'll tell you more. All we can tell you at the moment is that she had been brought up in a well-to-do family and she's fit and well." News of a granddaughter would just complicate things and could wait.

The DNA tests were duly administered. The inevitable outcome was that Sarah Jane Forester was identified as Sonya Ferguson, daughter of Karen and Sean Ferguson. All she retained from her past life were the initials of her name.

CHAPTER FIFTEEN

It was only with difficulty that Alice Walker persuaded Sonya/Sarah to meet her mother. More than a mere meeting was in the air. Although it had not been mentioned Sonya/Sarah was conscious of the fact that restoration to her "true" family might be in issue.

"I don't want to meet her. I have a mother already – she's quite enough."

Sarah/Sonya was almost gratified when the car pulled up outside a mean terrace house in the poorest part of town. There was no way she could possibly live here nor that any reasonable person might expect her to. She nevertheless got out of the car and approached the front door (God knows when it last had a coat of paint!) with Alice. Alice knocked on the door. She had hardly finished when it was flung open and Karen rushed out, arms spread, and embraced an extremely unwilling Sonya.

"Sonya!" she exclaimed. "At last! I knew you'd come back. I've searched for years – never stopped; never gave up hope."

She attempted to plant a kiss on Sonya's cheek but Sonya flinched away.

"My baby, my baby," exclaimed Karen, "You're my baby; I'm your mother."

Sarah/Sonya had had little enough time to avoid this onslaught. In the first few seconds, she noted a head of grey hair – an attempt might have

140

been made to neaten it up but if so it had failed. And the smell when she felt herself pulled into the embrace – a combination of God knows what ingredients but certainly including rancid cooking fat and stale tobacco. This woman wore no make-up other than some bright red lipstick, hastily and carelessly applied, so it seemed. Her clothes were worn and shabby. Sonya did not appreciate that Karen had put on her best things for the occasion.

They went inside – the front door opened straight into what the occupants described as "the parlour".

There were occupants – two of them. Sonya had been given a briefing. Her mother was living with her grandmother since her parents had split up. It had indeed been Sonya's first impression when the door was flung open that the hag confronting her must be her grandmother but it was now clear that she was the crone sitting on the worn sofa.

"Come in, come in," urged Karen, her remarks addressed to her long-lost daughter as though Alice did not exist. She made another attempt to embrace Sonya but Sonya evaded her arms. Karen was a bit perplexed. She had assumed without really thinking about it that Sonya would be as ecstatic about returning to her family, as they were to get her back. But Sonya was not obviously pleased to be back. Karen tried to understand:

"I know. You don't recognise me, do you? How

could you? You were only a tiny baby when you were stolen. How could you remember me?" Attempting to introduce some cheer into a cheerless atmosphere, Karen continued, "but we'll get to know one another again when you've been here a while."

"What!" thought Sonya – "'been here a while!' What's this?" It had occurred to her that she might be expected to return to live with her birth mother but it was still shocking to realise that that was what was now in prospect. She had hoped it was just a matter of meeting her and saying 'hello' but it now seemed clear that that hope was forlorn. "How fucking stupid of me," she thought. She turned to Alice:

"What's going on here? I've come. I never wanted to, you know that. What's all this about 'been here a while'?"

Karen and her mother looked on, not willing to understand what they were hearing. Karen interjected:

"You're home now, darling. This is your home. We are a family again. I'm your mother!"

Spoiled, selfish and insensitive, Sonya cruelly retorted, "You're not my mother. I already have a mother. I only came here to see you because they insisted," gesturing towards Alice. "I shouldn't have come," she added, heading for the front door.

"Wait Sarah... Sonya," intervened Alice. "This is your mother – your true mother," and, with a gesture towards the crone occupying the sofa, "and this is your real grandmother. You know how it is."

Sarah knew how it was but she also knew that it was not what she wanted. She was not going to have it. She opened the door and, without a word or a gesture, left the house and headed off up the street, she knew not where. She only knew that her world, with all the charm and comforts, which attended the well-to-do middle class, was somewhere else. It was not here in these dingy streets amongst these grubby people.

Alice uttered a hasty apology to Karen and her mother:

"Don't worry. She's upset. It's all very strange for her. She'll come round," and dashed after Sarah.

She caught her up. "Sarah! You can't just walk out like that. She's your mother. She's been searching for you for nearly seventeen years!"

"I can't help that. I don't know her. I don't want to know her. I didn't ask to be stolen but I was. I'm a Forester. They are my family..." adding, after a moment's thought, "for better or worse."

Alice continued to remonstrate but clearly Sarah was having none of it.

Over the ensuing days, Karen pestered Alice for news.

"She'll come round, I'm sure. Just give her time. It's all a great shock to her," Alice sought to calm her. But there was no assurance that Alice could give that would pacify Karen. Alice was eventually obliged to admit that Sonya adamantly refused to revisit, let alone reside with her true mother and grandmother. Slowly, reluctantly, imperceptibly, Karen came to face the truth. Sonya would never come back.

Three weeks later, at 3:00 a.m., Karen crept downstairs into the kitchen. She made a cup of tea and rolled a cigarette. She lit it and smoked it as she drank the tea. Then she fetched two cushions from the parlour and went back into the kitchen. There, she knelt down in front of the gas oven, placed one cushion in its base. She switched on the gas, turned on her back, leaned her head back on the cushion in the oven and arranged the second cushion as best she could to prevent an escape of gas. She was dead within minutes.

CHAPTER SIXTEEN

Once Sarah's true identity was revealed, Kate's position became perilous. The police immediately revisited her and put it to her that her story about the foundling on the doorstep was a pack of lies. She, however, stuck to her guns. The abductor, whoever she was, had obviously changed her mind when she realised what she had done and palmed off the responsibility onto Kate. Let them prove otherwise.

But the baby had been seen disappearing down the road in a "flashy car". The note left in the bassinet, they put it to her, was barely literate, not likely to have been written by a clearly well-to-do woman, able to drive an expensive car.

"I can tell you plenty of your so-called 'well-to-do' women driving 'flashy cars' who got where they are only because they're good fucks," Kate retorted.

She still stuck to her guns.

Everybody was sure she was the perpetrator. The "foundling" tale was a load of nonsense. All they lacked was evidence. They had practically nothing to go on. Unless they could extract a confession there seemed to be no way forward and Kate was well aware of the consequences of a confession. There was not even enough to constitute anything like a *prima facie* case to send to the Crown Prosecution Service. As the weeks went by, it looked more and more like the case that Kate would get away with it once again.

She was, said Kate on the occasion of her next meeting with her mother, in the clear. This was perhaps optimistic but that was how it had begun to look. When Rosalie was next in contact with George and the topic arose Rosalie told him that that was how things appeared to be. The police simply had no evidence either of Kate being involved in the abduction or of her foundling alibi being false.

George alone had reason to believe that it might be false. Had his sister shown any inclination towards a reconciliation he might have hesitated but she had not. She had drawn up the battle lines. He was not going to lose the fight. He talked it over with Val and she was adamant. The poor child's parents had endured sixteen years of agony. Kate's rejection of her own brother had utterly alienated Val. Kate should pay, reconciliation or not. It was, for her, unthinkable that Sonya's parents should be denied retribution after all the years of suffering.

George duly contacted the Birmingham police. He told them exactly what he had witnessed. His initial reaction was one of surprise at their scepticism but he responded to their request to meet them in Birmingham. Val drove him to Dinard for the flight to Southampton where he hired a car to take him to Birmingham. At police headquarters, he found himself confronted by Detective-Inspector Alyn Probert, who was accompanied by Sergeant Joanne

Helby from Warwick. She knew as much about the case as anyone.

Probert began the questioning. It seemed to George more like an interrogation but he was used to that:

"You know where we stand with the investigation into the abduction of Sonya Ferguson, I believe."

"I think so, yes!" responded George.

"We think your sister, Kate Forester, took her. You appreciate that?"

"I do, indeed."

"And you want to give evidence against your sister?"

"I hardly 'want' to. I've thought long and hard about it. Why? Do you think I should keep quiet about it?"

"No, no," intervened Joanne. "It's just a bit odd, that's all. A brother giving evidence that might send his sister to prison for a long spell."

"Well, my wife and I thought about it. Obviously, I don't like the idea but we were thinking about the poor parents. We just thought they had suffered long enough."

"Anyway," continued Probert, "we gather that you can help us establish that your sister took the baby."

"Yes, it's as I told you over the 'phone. I saw her arrive at the house and take in the baby and all the baby stuff."

"Yes, well she admits to finding the baby, but two days after the abduction. You say you saw her on the day of the abduction?"

"I did, yes."

"Are you sure you're not mistaken? Could it have been two days later? It was a long time ago."

"I'm certain of the date. It was on the day I was released from prison."

Eyebrows were raised when he assured them that he was certain of the date and of the reason for his certainty. They had not realised they were dealing with a convicted criminal. Not always, they found themselves thinking, the most reliable of witnesses.

"I was waiting in the road for her to come home. I had nowhere else to go. Minutes before Kate arrived home, I heard the news of the abduction on the car radio. It was the main news headline you know. I wasn't certain, of course. Could have been a co-incidence. But I'm absolutely certain about one thing. It may have been a "foundling" but it was not being delivered on the doorstep two days later. A baby, some baby, had arrived, in Kate's 'flashy car', less than three hours after baby Sonya had been snatched."

"Why didn't you say something at the time?" asked Joanne.

"I've said, I wasn't certain. And in any case, the last thing I wanted to do was risk getting involved. As you may have gathered, I went to prison a few times when I was younger. I reckoned you lot would just assume I had something to do with it."

Eyebrows were again raised, but they had to acknowledge that he had a point.

"I got away as fast as I could."

The fact that it was the very day on which he had been released from prison was the clincher. The police went over the ground with George again and confirmed his release date. They had never believed the "foundling" story and were now confirmed in their scepticism.

Kate was arrested and duly appeared before magistrates the next day when she refused to plead but a "not guilty" plea was entered and she was committed for trial at the Crown Court in six weeks' time. She fulminated inwardly at her betrayal by her own brother but she recognised that it was all over. She did not bother to contact her solicitor.

Over the ensuing six weeks, Kate went over her position again and again. She could see no way that she might be acquitted. She pondered the idea of going abroad – to France, maybe, to the *manoir*, but realised that all that would amount to was hanging about for the service of the European arrest warrant. Other ideas were entertained and dismissed – a world cruise; a new life under a new name in the Caribbean or elsewhere. But none of this either appealed to or convinced her. They would catch up with her sooner or later. And in any case, her old life was over and she was too old to start a new one.

On the evening of the day before her trial, Kate went down to the cellar and brought up two bottles of *Pouilly Fume Ladoucette*. She went to the kitchen. The eye-level electric double oven did not offer her Karen's way out.

She opened the first bottle and poured a glass. She went to the fridge and, rummaging about, found the remnants of some ancient foie gras and a half-eaten slab of *bleu d'Auvergne*. She could not be bothered to toast bread or even butter it. She finished the first glass of the wine and poured another. She ate what little she could bother with of the pate and cheese. After all, there seemed little point in eating. She switched on the television but did not even register what was showing. She finished the second glass and took the empty glass and the rest of the bottle into the conservatory where she poured another glass. She switched on the tape-player – it had a collection of her favourite pieces but she heard little. She finished the first bottle.

She went to the kitchen and brought out the second bottle. Searching for a corkscrew in a drawer in the dresser she found an old box of Cuban cheroots. They had not been near a humidor for years. She rarely smoked but lit one anyway – a last act of pathetic defiance. In the circumstances, the risk of self-harm from tobacco did not loom too large. The cigar did not taste of much; it neither pleased nor offended her. She found a corkscrew and opened the second bottle.

It was just after midnight, the day of her trial, when she went out onto the terrace taking glass, bottle and cigars with her. It was a clear, bitterly cold night and an icy breeze was blowing but by this time she was somewhat anaesthetised by the first bottle. She nevertheless started to shiver. She poured another glass and lit another cigar.

The sound of Ashkenazi's piano floated out of the conservatory door. By now, she was shivering violently. Slowly, she undressed placing blouse, skirt and then underwear on the metal grill of a chair and sat down. A bit ridiculous, she thought, worrying about her arse sticking to the freezing metal grill at such a time.

The music switched to Tchaikovsky's sixth symphony, the *Pathetique.*

She was by now shaking so much that she could hardly raise the next two glasses to her lips without spilling the wine. How awful to waste the *Ladoucette* she said to herself and laughed out loud at her stupidity.

But then, quietly, she shook no more. She heard the start of the last movement of the *Pathetique* but she never heard the end. She felt numb. Then she felt nothing.

CHAPTER SEVENTEEN

Sarah never went back to Warwick. She would probably never have done so anyway but a letter from one "Angela Thomas," clinched things. It read:

"I hesitate to write this – I feel very guilty and I think I ought to apologise to you. I do apologise; I'm very sorry that things have turned out this way. But you are entitled to know that Tom has been unfaithful to you – with me.

"I was, and am, very fond of him. That is my only excuse. But I have come to believe that as far as he is concerned, it is nothing but sex.

"I hope I am doing the right thing. He should not be deceiving you.

"Yours sincerely,

"Angela Thomas."

This letter was the last brick in the wall. Their unencumbered life together when they were young had been a fertile soil in which love had flourished profusely. Now, almost suddenly it seemed, nothing was easy, nothing was certain anymore. The baby had made things very difficult. Angela's letter had made them impossible.

Thinking about her situation, Sarah perceived that she had four options:

1. She (and the baby) could return to live with her mother and grandmother. This possibility she had categorically rejected. It was hard to

imagine a less congenial environment.

2. She could return to Warwick and live with Tom. She was already wholly unenamoured of this prospect even before she received Angela's letter. That had clinched it.

3. She could stay where she was – for the time being. She found living with Vittoria and Bella, and without her "mother" and "brother" an altogether more congenial prospect than any of the alternatives. But it was only "for the time being." Her mother's estate would have to be wound up. Probably the house would be sold. And as far as she could see, Vittoria and Bella, as well as her, faced eviction and unemployment.

4. There might be the possibility of becoming a member of her father's new family. Alice had been pressing her to visit them and get to know them. Sean and Vicky were quite keen to meet her but her experience of the visit to her mother and grandmother has chastened her and made her cautious and apprehensive. She was, she realised, going to have to grit her teeth and consider that possibility. She was encouraged by Alice's assurance that she would be welcome and Alice's description of the Barn and the family, which inhabited it, were in marked contrast with her experience of her grandmother's place.

There was another and more pressing problem. What was she going to live on? Theretofore, there had been no problem. They had been very well provided for by Kate but that source had dried up. As a daughter, Sarah would have inherited a half of Kate's millions. It now looked, however, as if Kate had ultimately disowned her. Under the new Will, apart from legacies of ten thousand pounds each to Vittoria and Bella, everything went to Tom, Kate's only true child. Vittoria and Bella, as well as Sarah, thought this very harsh.

In the event, Tom agreed to pay slightly more than he was legally-obliged to in maintenance to Sarah for her and their daughter. Rosalie, meanwhile, obliged and gratified to acknowledge a great-grandchild and warming somewhat towards its mother arranged to pay a generous monthly allowance to Sarah for her and the child. So that problem at least was eventually solved.

Rosalie had had to endure decades of near-solitude at The Poplars. Peter's early death had committed her to an early and prolonged widowhood. For some years thereafter, her family and friends had kept loneliness at bay. Then the children had left home one by one. Alex had emigrated to British Columbia. She would have retained friends and coffee mornings, occasional invitations out to dinner and bridge would have ensured companionship but then George's misdemeanours had slowly dissolved her social circle to the point where it hardly existed any longer.

Tom's conviction of unlawful carnal knowledge of a child finished the job. It had resulted in his exclusion from Warwick. It was a consequence he had not thought of. It meant that there was no longer any particular point in living in the flat in Warwick. Obviously, however, if he was no longer to live there, the question arose 'where was he to live?' No-one wanted him back at home. Sarah did not want him there; he did not want to be there with Sarah. Vittoria and Bella would have put up with his return without greatly welcoming it.

He ended up with his grandmother at The Poplars. It was more than big enough for them both. Furthermore, it framed a life for him albeit perhaps only in the immediate future. At school, he had proved to be quite adept at hitting a ball with a stick and the golf course was just round the corner. He had assumed that membership would be a formality and was somewhat taken aback to be told by an elderly committee member, James Hendick, an erstwhile friend of his grandfather, that consideration of his application had been deferred:

"I had hoped it would be a formality," Hendick told him after the meeting "but there was a bit of humming and hawing. I tried to explain the circumstances – your not really being a sex offender and all – but they decided to postpone a decision to the next meeting. Don't worry; I'll have a private chat with one or two of them. It will probably work out alright."

It was only then that it really dawned on Tom that in the eyes of the world he was a convicted paedophile.

This was, it is true, a rather harsh judgment but it carried weight and, but for the Forester fortune, might have turned out to be a serious disability. Events were, however, on his side. The club had, just over a year previously, taken the historic step of admitting women to membership. This was, incidentally, not the first reluctant trudge towards liberalism. Over twenty-five years previously, they had resolved to admit Jews.

There it was. The women could play through the week from Monday morning to Friday lunchtime provided, that is, they could find somewhere to change. Home, the car, or a mixture of the two had to suffice. The men's changing room was, furthermore, in a rather shabby condition and could do with refurbishment.

When, at its next meeting, Hendick put it to the committee that he might be able to negotiate a solution to these problems, everyone listened. "Young Forester" (he was not really a paedophile, you know; not the usual sort... an unfortunate business with his sister, well, his foster sister) wished to make

156

a generous donation to the club. He would pick up the bill for new changing rooms for the men. And, no, young Forester and made it clear that this offer was not conditional on his being admitted as a member. His grandfather had been a keen member; he though it appropriate that he should do something.

It solved the problem. The women could have the old changing rooms – somewhat refurbished, of course. Hendick's "Don't know what they'll make of the urinals" brought forth chuckles, lightened the tone and ensured that Tom's application for membership was, this time round, favourably viewed.

Tom soon became adept at the game. He did little else. Playing a round every day, usually ended with a session with newfound friends in the Men's Bar (there was another bar, which the women could use. No need to carry reforms to excess). He soon brought his handicap down to fifteen and he once came second in the weekly handicap event.

Through his new acquaintances in the Mens' bar he found a ready solution to his personal needs in the company of Charlene. They had a regular arrangement. He would pick her up; they would go out to dinner, then back to The Poplars. Charlene's appearance at breakfast initially surprised Rosalie but she soon became used to it happening once or twice a week. After some months, she took Tom aside and asked him:

"Charlene seems like a really nice girl. Why

don't you make an honest woman of her?"

She was a nice girl. She was more than merely nice. She was beautiful and personable. What Rosalie never realised, however, was that Charlene did very well amongst her clientele in Altrincham and Prestbury, many of them professional footballers and all of them highly-paid, by being a non-honest woman and neither she nor Tom wanted to change this. They saw no point in disabusing Rosalie of her misconception and she remained subject to it for the whole of their relationship.

This was not Rosalie's only misconception. She was now in her eighties and Tom began noticing things. He arrived home from the Golf Club on one occasion to find her wandering around the kitchen muttering to herself.

"What's the matter Gran?" he asked.

"Can't find the damned teapot. Wanted to make myself a cup of tea but don't know where the bloody thing is," Rosalie had explained.

Tom spotted it, by the kettle. It was hot and it was full.

"Here it is, Gran. You've already made the tea."

"No I haven't. I couldn't find the pot."

"It's here Gran, ready to pour."

Perplexed, Rosalie could only manage, "Oh."

Tom wondered, not for the first time, if all was well with Rosalie. He wondered again when, coming home from golf once more, he entered the house and yelled out, "Hello Gran."

She emerged from the sitting room into the hall, stared at him and to his astonishment asked, "Who are you? What are you doing in my house?"

"It's me, Gran, Tom."

"Tom?" she queried and then, only after a silence, "Ah, yes, Tom. Sorry; stupid of me."

Tom briefly wondered if it was just her eyesight but that had never been a problem. He wondered about it overnight and the next morning broached the subject at breakfast:

"You know you didn't recognise me when I came home yesterday."

Rosalie hesitated, then said, "Yes, I know. Funny thing…" then continued, "A few funny things have been happening lately."

"Yes, I'd noticed," added Tom. "Do you think you're alright? How about letting Doctor Hurley check you over?"

"That might be a good idea," admitted Rosalie.

The result of the visit to Doctor Hurley was a diagnosis of dementia. It was still early days and recent advances had raised the possibility of slowing down its progress. But the prognosis was inevitably somewhat negative.

"Don't forget, you're in your eighties now. You can't expect to avoid what often comes with ageing. And it's early days. Try to think positively about it.

You probably have years of happy life ahead of you. It's a problem, yes, but don't worry about it. Enjoy life."

But Tom did worry about it. His motives were not entirely unselfish. What would it be like if he couldn't rely on her to look after him properly – do his washing, cook his meals? But he was also very fond of her. Something had to be done.

He had been wondering about selling his mother's house. It had become his when Kate's estate was wound up. He had put off deciding out of consideration for Vittoria and Bella, not wholly altruistically for they were caring for Sarah and the baby. There was now, however, the problem of caring for his grandmother. The dementia might still be only in its early stages, but it was not going to go away, was it.

In this context it occurred to Tom to wonder if perhaps it might be time to sell the house. This would create a problem for Vittoria and Bella but he had a solution to offer, if they were interested. He might ask Vittoria and Bella if they would be prepared to move to The Poplars to serve that Forester household. Rosalie's cooking, never a strong point, was an occasional victim of her dementia and their temporary house-keeping arrangements involving a couple of somewhat unreliable girls from the town were not satisfactory.

When it came to the crunch Vittoria and Bella

were more than happy to make the move to The Poplars. It seemed natural; they had been with Foresters for sixteen or seventeen years and were, in a way, now part of the larger family. And unemployment accompanied by the need to embark on new careers had no appeal. Tom accordingly put the house on the market. There was only one problem – Sarah and the baby. What would happen to her? Neither Rosalie nor Tom liked the idea of having her at the Poplars. In any case, they were providing well for her, financially speaking. Surely she could sort herself out even if she was only seventeen.

Sarah had made it abundantly clear that she would rather die (as, it occurred to her, had both her mothers) than contemplate life with her grandmother in the decrepit terrace house in the poorest part of town. She was now obliged to take seriously the prospect of whatever sort of life, if any, might be offered by her father and his new family.

She had been under pressure from Alice to visit them but had managed thus far to put such a meeting off. Her encounter with her mother and grandmother had ill-disposed her to any more such visits to her father and his new family. She did not know them and found it hard to conceive of herself having any place there. Now, almost out of necessity, she agreed to go and see them.

CHAPTER EIGHTEEN

Sean Ferguson had never forgotten his daughter Sonya but he did not remember her in the same way as had Karen, her mother. By the time Sonya re-emerged from the darkness of her abduction, Sean had been leading a new life for many years. He and Vicky, the young widow whom he had met at work, had started a new family and by the time Sonya re-appeared on the scene, Luke and Janet were already in the fourth and fifth forms respectively at the local comprehensive school.

The intervening years had seen the second Ferguson family progress. After four years as foreman and following upon the retirement of the existing manager, Sean was promoted to that role. Vicky, too, had made progress in her career. She was now assistant director of the cosmetics department in a large out-of-town department store.

The birth of a boy and a girl coupled with the increase in the family's income had prompted a move to a barn and stables which had been part of a farm just four miles west of the town. Sean's share of the proceeds of sale of the terrace house had financed the purchase of the unimproved farm buildings.

Sean himself had set about the conversion, which they financed wholly out of income. The family had had to live for a while in temporary rented accommodation but not for long. Within three months the four of them moved into one large room and a bathroom and kitchen as soon as Sean was able to equip these rooms with the basic amenities. The four of them lived and ate at one end of the former barn and slept at the other end. Sean, working all evenings and weekends, developed a second living room, three bedrooms and another bathroom over the ensuing eighteen months at the end of which they were the owners of a handsome barn conversion, free of mortgage.

Alice eventually succeeded in persuading Sarah to visit her father and his new family. Sarah had finally come round to the view that if the offer for her to live with the Fergusons was made it might well be her best option. Thus it was to the Ferguson barn conversion that the Alice delivered Sarah/Sonya to meet her father for the first time in over sixteen years. The meeting was in stark contrast with Sonya's encounter with her birth mother. Sonya/Sarah had had a surfeit of mothers but she had never had a father in her second life as Kate's daughter. The "Andrew Blake" on her birth certificate had nothing whatever to do with her, either genetically or socially.

The meeting was amicable if only because all, other than the social worker, were in agreement. Sean was bemused to meet his lost daughter for the first time in all those years. He found her attractive and well-turned-out but suddenly realised that he was looking at her as a stranger. Guiltily, he admitted to himself that he had long ago accepted that she was dead. He had mourned her and moved on.

But at the same time, he realised that he did not lack feelings for her. He was her father. This young lady was his daughter. He felt a strange type of nostalgia and a willing benevolence towards her. He found himself pondering the question whether he should welcome her back, problematic because he now had a new family and the addition of Sonya and a granddaughter might cause all sorts of problems.

Vicky as it turned out was not a problem; quite the opposite. Although she had only come onto the scene after Sonya's abduction she felt very sorry for her and was, unlike her husband, more than willing to welcome her into the new Ferguson home.

For her part, Sarah/Sonya, had not, as she had feared, found this Ferguson family environment repulsive as she had her mother's; the contrary was the case. Although she had registered it as a possibility, she had, until very recently, not thus far entertained the idea that they might ask her to join them. Despite the social worker's urgings, which came near to threats at one point, Sarah was determined and unwavering as to who was to decide her future. It was she herself. They could take her into care if they insisted but they would not be able to keep her there. Her options had, however, become very restricted although, she was now forced to recognise, again becoming part of her father's and her stepmother's family had become perhaps the best of them if, that is, they were willing to accept her and her child.

The initial visit to the barn had really been nothing more than a reconnaissance foray, for both sides. It had not, however, as had her only visit to her birth mother's home, repelled her – the contrary was the case.

Largely due to Vicky's initiative, other visits to the barn followed and Sonya/Sarah began to feel more and more relaxed there. In particular, she came to enjoy Vicky's company in a way in which she had never previously enjoyed the companionship of a female friend. It was a relationship, which was highlighted by the last months of her life with the baby in Warwick when Tom had been absent much of the time (surreptitiously shagging that cow next door, she reminded herself).

So it was that when things came to a crunch and Tom decided to sell the house with Vittoria and Bella happily making the move to The Poplars, Sarah/Sonya's fourth option, living with her father and his family at the barn increased greatly in attraction. When, visiting them yet again, she put her dilemma to them, it produced the result that she had, without admitting it to herself, been hoping for.

"I shall find somewhere," she had said. "Tom is paying me maintenance and Rosalie, his grandmother, has promised to top it up substantially.

And that means 'a lot' – she's rolling in it; worth millions. I should be able to rent a flat or something…"

"Nonsense!" said Vicky. You must come here. We're your family now." Sean entered a cautious qualified assent:

"Of course, but we shall have some sorting out to do. We only have the three bedrooms, I'm not sure how we'd be able to arrange things."

Vicky soon straightened him out:

"No. It's not a problem. Seamus will be going to university in the autumn so there'll be his room initially. And then you can get on with doing up the stables. You've been on about it long enough. It's time you got it sorted."

And so it was. Again working practically every evening and most weekends, Sean carved two further rooms and a bathroom out of the stables. Before Seamus arrived back for Christmas, Sonya/Sarah had her own rooms for herself and the baby.

There remained one minor matter, easily resolved. On her visits to the barn, she had been referred to sometimes as Sonya and sometimes as Sarah. She finally got round to it:

"Can we settle this business of what I'm called once and for all, please? I don't mind being called Sonya. But I've always been Sarah and that's what I'd like to be called, if nobody objects. I don't really mind which. What I really don't like is being called both or either."

Sean was the only one who might have wished to call his daughter Sonya but it turned out that he didn't mind one way or the other, so Sarah it was, as it had been for all her conscious life.

Once the baby was weaned, Sarah was free to resume an education of a sort. It was not Jevington but evening classes at the local technical college eventually enabled her to come away with some respectable GCSE results. She might have gone on to take A-Levels, but then she might also have become the first female Archbishop of Canterbury but she lacked the desire to do either. She made female friends through acquaintances of Vicky and settled into a life of motherhood, coffee mornings and shopping. Her small share of the Forester fortune enabled her to further these activities without worrying unduly about cost. It may be that she will eventually meet some "nice young man" who is willing to take on someone else's child. It happens, but it has not happened yet.

CHAPTER NINETEEN

Three years after Sean acquired "Ferguson Tyres and Exhausts" he took on Jack Hepworth, a lad fresh from the comprehensive school, who had managed to get an A in his IT A-level whilst failing at everything else. It turned out that he was as much a genius with computers as he was a dunce at repairing and fitting tyres and exhausts.

A regular customer had come in for two new tyres and in the course of conversation with Sean whilst he waited he moaned:

"Fucking petrol gauge has stopped working again. Don't know whether the tank's full or empty. I'll have to take it into them again. It'll cost a fucking fortune but they're the only people who seem to have any idea."

"Which is why they can charge you a fortune," offered Sean, then, inspired, said:

"We've just taken on a young lad here; he's computer mad. Why don't we let him take a look at it?"

"Why not?" was the reply.

Jack fixed the fault in minutes.

It was a seminal moment. It gave birth to the idea of adding electrics to the traditional tyre and exhaust business. Practically all cars nowadays relied on computers. They regularly went wrong and it was one repair, which eluded the skills of all but the very

168

best of DIY owners.

It took Sean and Jack much longer than they had anticipated to acquire the skills necessary for the addition of the full range of 'electrics' to the 'tyre and exhausts' of the existing business. But they got there in the end. Sean sent Jack to the Technical College to follow courses in car maintenance during the day and attended evening classes himself where he sometimes ran across his daughter Sarah.

"Ferguson Tyres Exhausts and Electrics" was a rather cumbersome name for the business. It was Vicky who came up with "Ferguson Carfix" and the firm was duly rebranded.

It soon became apparent that the firm's existing premises were too small and when a shop next door fell vacant, "Ferguson Carfix" acquired a ten-year lease the additional space being devoted largely to the electrics.

Within a year it became clear that with the addition of electrical and especially computer work the profits of the firm were burgeoning. It was again Vicky who noticed an advertisement for the sale of a garage and workshop on the far side of town. The previous owner had relied largely on fuel sales but they had fallen victim to competition from a newly established superstore just two hundred yards up the road and he was losing money hand over fist. He was anxious to sell but pessimistic about doing so. The price was "ripe".

Ferguson Carfix's existing premises were becoming inadequate for the expanding business and they were able to do a deal which satisfied both parties. They kept on the car fuel business. They raised prices, sold less and managed just about to break even but that did not matter. And they could, whenever they wished, abandon that part of the business. The core business, especially the electrics branch, thrived and Sean and Vicky decided to incorporate and limit their liability. The shares were divided equally between them - a recipe for deadlock which has not, however, so far occurred.

Some months later, Vicky, again, noticed that similar premises were for sale in a nearby town. It was almost exactly the same situation again – new hypermarket offering discounted prices on motor fuel; local service station put out of business.

For Ferguson Carfix It represented an opportunity for expansion but it was a big step to take. They would be operating in a new and unfamiliar business environment where their name was nothing like as well-known as in Burton. They would have to borrow more money - but it could be the start of a business empire.

The family discussed it at length over much of several evenings. Sean and Seamus were keen on the idea, but Sarah and especially Vicky were less convinced.

They could raise money on the security of the

barn. Who could tell? The brand might take off nationwide. They were doing very well as they were but if they took the plunge and fortune smiled on them they might end up making millions.

Published by

www.publishandprint.co.uk

#0049 - 020318 - C0 - 210/148/9 - PB - DID2137253